T0123205

DEAD
SPIDER

DEAD SPIDER

A NOVEL

VICTORIA HOUSTON

Gallery Books

New York London Toronto Sydney New Delhi

Gallery Books
An Imprint of Simon & Schuster, Inc.
1230 Avenue of the Americas
New York, NY 10020

First Gallery Books trade paperback edition JUNE 2017

GALLERY BOOKS and colophon are registered trademarks of Simon and Schuster, Inc.

For information about special discounts for bulk purchases, please contact Simon & Schuster Special Sales at 1-866-506-1949 or business@simonandschuster.com.

The Simon & Schuster Speakers Bureau can bring authors to your live event. For more information or to book an event contact the Simon & Schuster Speakers Bureau at 1-866-248-3049 or visit our website at www.simonspeakers.com.

Interior design by Colleen Cunningham

Manufactured in the United States of America

10 9 8 7 6 5 4 3 2 1

Library of Congress Cataloging-in-Publication Data has been applied for.

ISBN 978-1-5072-0456-6
ISBN 978-1-4405-9881-4 (ebook)

FOR ROGER: MY WISE, DEAR FRIEND.
YOU ARE MISSED BY MANY.

"It is easy to look, but learning to see is a more gradual business, and it sneaks up on you unconsciously, by stealth."

—ROBERT HUGHES

CHAPTER ONE

"Erin, I am too old for this," shouted Dr. Paul Osborne as he struggled to be heard over loudspeakers blasting "Who Let the Dogs Out?" With a shake of her head his daughter sent a questioning smile his way. It was obvious she hadn't heard a word he'd said.

The noise level was too frustrating. After all, Erin, his youngest daughter and the mother of his three grandchildren, was sitting in a folding lawn chair *less than ten feet away*—and she still couldn't hear him? Raising his voice, Osborne repeated himself while wondering what demented individual insisted on blaring this same raucous song at the highest decibel possible at what seemed like every single game his grandkids played whether hockey, basketball, soccer—even today's fishing tournament. For heaven's sake.

"Hang in there, Dad," said Erin, managing to be heard over the pounding rhythms. "The winners will be announced any minute now. Keep your fingers crossed; our Mason is a finalist in the muskie division."

Relaxing back into his lawn chair, legs crossed and one hand cradling a can of ginger ale fresh from the cooler, Osborne gazed across the lawn to the wide dock extending alongside the boat landing behind the Tall Pines Tavern. Thanks to savvy owners dedicated to sponsoring volleyball and snowshoe baseball tournaments paired with an oversized parking lot, the tavern had become the go-to site for Loon Lake events likely to draw a crowd. And it never hurt that a cold beer on tap was never more than a few hundred feet away.

He had picked a spot for them to sit on a slight rise, away from the busy booths where young and old stood in line clamoring for sodas, cheese curds, and hot dogs, but close enough to the water that they could see the action on the award stage. Or so he had thought. He hadn't planned on so many eager parents and grandparents milling in front of the stage where the awards would be handed out and all prepared to hold cell phones over their heads to take photos. Some were so intent on the proceedings they were taking photos of the judges.

Today was the last day of the Loon Lake Youth Fishing Tournament and the awards ceremony was set to begin shortly, though the judging was still underway. From where he was sitting, Osborne could see the nodding of official heads, which indicated that the winners of the panfish and walleye contests had been decided. But that left the winners in his granddaughter's category, i.e., youngsters competing to catch muskies—fish larger than most of them—still to be determined. Only then could the awards ceremony begin. *And hopefully soon,* thought Osborne in frustration as dozens of people continued to flow toward the stage and further obscure his vision.

In recent years this tournament for anglers between the ages of ten and sixteen had become a highlight of the summer, drawing competitors and spectators from across the Northwoods, not to mention television crews and sports magazines. There was even a rumor that a scout for one of the national walleye tournaments was in the crowd.

Bleachers lining the lakeside were packed with people of all ages. The grassy berm and paved biking trail that ran behind the bleachers was studded with an overflow of strollers and buggies, old folks in wheelchairs, and hyperactive youngsters on bikes and trikes. Teenage boys showing off their pickups buzzed in and out of the parking lot, revving engines, squealing tires, and tossing firecrackers in the direction of admiring girls.

A warm mid-June Sunday highlighted with kegs of beer and soda on ice and the aroma of fresh-grilled bratwurst added up to a recipe for a community high: Good spirits ran rampant.

"Man, you gotta shoot yourself in the foot not to have a good time today," Osborne's neighbor, Ray Pradt, had quipped earlier as he and Osborne had joined other volunteers to set out folding chairs and erect a stage for the awards ceremony.

Ray, a local fishing guide who had also volunteered to coach the kids in the muskie fishing division, was not exaggerating for once: The day could not have been more perfect with temperatures in the low eighties, the sun high, the sky cloudless, and just enough breeze to keep the mosquitoes away.

While he waited for the annoying song to end and the awards ceremony to begin, Osborne studied the crowd. Though he was three years retired from his dental practice, thirty years of exploring local mouths had made him familiar with many of the faces in the crowd. He knew most of the men and women manning the booths sponsored by the Jaycees, the Lions Club, and the Rotary.

Then there were the picnic tables in the booth designated for the elderly from the Senior Center—he knew everyone there. Even the playground area with its slides, swings, and sandbox where toddlers were being watched by teenage volunteers from the YMCA held people he might have treated when they were kids.

The event was not just a family gathering. Local businesses were eager to participate. Ralph's Sporting Goods had a booth as did the Chamber of Commerce, the Loon Lake Pub, and the local pasty shop. But the sponsor plastered across the awning covering the stage was Pfeiffer's Fishing, Golf, and Shooting Sports.

The tournament was Chuck Pfeiffer's baby. His company had launched it and over the years Pfeiffer's made sure all the food and beverages for the participants and their families were free.

Chuck could afford to be generous. It was twenty-five years ago to the day almost since he had taken over a tiny two-aisle sporting goods shop into which its owner had crammed fishing rods, lures, shotguns, deer rifles, and bug spray. Chuck changed the name from McClellan's to Pfeiffer's, upgraded the inventory, added golf gear, expanded into the space next door—and morphed from one small shop on Loon Lake's Main Street into a juggernaut of over seventy stores in three states. Today Chuck Pfeiffer was considered by many to be the richest man in Wisconsin.

Local residents were proud to say that even though Chuck Pfeiffer could afford to fish anywhere in the world he never missed their annual Loon Lake Youth Fishing Tournament. And a cluster of chairs and tables in a booth under a bright yellow awning had been roped off for the Pfeiffer contingent of family and staff.

To Osborne's relief, the music came to an abrupt halt and a voice over the sound system alerted the crowd that the ceremony would begin in less than fifteen minutes and to please be patient as they finalized the tournament results. He crossed his fingers on behalf of Mason, the granddaughter who had inherited his love of fishing. As bystanders crowded around the stage, forcing Osborne to stand up in order to get a better view, a familiar voice boomed in his ear:

"Hey, Doc, ya ol' razzbonya—what the hell you been up to? Did I hear you're retired? Livin' the dream these days? Say, why don't you come sit with me over in my booth there." The man pointed in the direction of the yellow awning. "Got a much better view."

Osborne turned toward the man who had appeared at his side. "Hey, Chuck—you're just in time to see if we've lost any kids to our 'shark of the north.'" Before Chuck could say more, Osborne put a finger to his lips and turned back toward the stage. Out of the corner of his eye, Osborne saw a young boy run up to Chuck and pull on his sleeve.

"My grandson," said Chuck with a hint of annoyance in his voice. "What is it, Brian? They're about to announce the winners. Aren't you supposed to be up on that stage?"

Osborne saw a tear slip down the boy's cheek. "I came in fourth, Grandpops," said the boy, his voice catching as if trying to choke back a sob.

"Fourth, huh. That's pretty darn good," said Osborne in a whisper loud enough for the boy to hear.

"No it isn't," said Chuck, his tone brusque as he yanked the kid's hand off his sleeve. "All that counts is first. I told you that. Remember? Now go find your mother."

Some things never change, thought Osborne. Chuck had been unpleasant years ago when they were young men sharing a deer shack with other men—and he was unpleasant today.

"We'll catch up later. Come by my place for a drink when all this baloney is over," said Chuck, waving as he sauntered in the direction of the yellow awning. Watching him go, Osborne pushed back memories of the young Chuck Pfeiffer: The day was too nice for dark thoughts.

As Chuck walked back to his booth, Erin pulled her chair over by Osborne's, but she had to stand, too, rising up on her tiptoes to see. As they both peered anxiously toward the stage a din erupted along the shoreline to the left of the dock where three teenage boys were huddled over a cache of fireworks they had smuggled into the celebration and had begun to fire off with glee. With an explosive burst a series of flaming balls and blue sparks flew high over the stage. Boom! Boom!

"Dad," said Erin, shouting to be heard over the explosions. "That's dangerous. Somebody better stop those kids before anyone gets hurt."

More booms, then the sound of a dull crack.

"Now that's enough," said Erin. "That sounded like a gunshot. I'm calling 911." Before she could reach for her cell phone, a distant siren could be heard.

"Hold on, Erin," said Osborne. "It's just fireworks. Look, one of the judges is running over there. I'm sure he'll put a lid on things."

Sure enough, within a minute, one of Loon Lake's fire trucks lumbered over the berm in the direction of the excitement. Osborne watched with amusement as the boys tried to salvage what was left of their incendiary toys and make an escape. No such luck.

———◆———

Mason tied for third place in the muskie division. Her grandfather and mother, along with her little brother, were thrilled. Forty-two kids had competed, which meant she had done very nicely. Chagrined at how Chuck Pfeiffer had been so wicked to his grandson, Osborne knew he overdid congratulating his granddaughter, but he couldn't help it.

After making sure Mason got a celebratory bratwurst followed by a two-scoop ice cream cone, Osborne helped Erin pack up the lawn chairs, the cooler, and Mason's fishing gear. The crowd was still milling in celebration, which was likely to last well into the evening, but for Osborne and his family it had been a long day.

They had just finished loading everything into the back of Erin's SUV when Osborne heard screams coming from the picnic area. "Dad, something's wrong," said Erin with a quick glance behind her to be sure Mason and Cody were nearby. "Looks like whatever it is might be over there," she pointed toward the yellow awning where the Pfeiffer crew had been sitting.

"You're right," said Osborne. "Doesn't sound good. Wait here with the kids while I see if someone needs help."

Minutes later, he knew there was nothing anyone could do. He reached for the cell phone he kept buttoned in the upper left pocket of his khaki shirt.

It rang once. "Chief Ferris," said the woman with whom he had enjoyed breakfast early that morning.

"Lewellyn, the richest man in Wisconsin just took a bullet in the brain."

CHAPTER TWO

Siren blaring, a squad car emblazoned "Loon Lake Police" sped into the parking lot behind the Tall Pines Tavern, forcing departing vehicles out of its way. A female figure in a khaki uniform with a distinctive mass of black-brown curls crowding her features jumped from the driver's seat and loped across a grassy swale toward the small crowd that had gathered near the yellow awning.

"Doc," said Loon Lake police chief Lewellyn Ferris as she reached the front ranks of onlookers, "have you called for an ambulance?" Osborne nodded.

"First thing, Chief. They should be here any minute. But I'm afraid it's too late for EMTs . . . "

Osborne stood aside watching as his close friend, fishing partner, and sometime boss dropped to her knees for a closer look at a man sitting with his head crooked slightly to the left. Leaning over her and keeping his voice low enough that only she could hear, Osborne pointed as he said, "He's gone. You can see where a bullet entered behind the right ear."

"Not much blood." Lew looked up at Osborne with a question in her eyes.

"No exit wound either. He died within seconds. I'm no firearms expert but sure looks to me like whoever pulled the trigger knew what they were doing. One thing we learned in the military—it is tough to kill someone with just one shot. Though I doubt we have professional snipers at a kids' fishing tournament."

Lew got to her feet. "Had to be someone who was able to get close."

"Yep."

Lew studied the body in the wooden Adirondack chair. With shoulders slumped and the head tilted forward and slightly to one side—had she not known better—she might have thought she was looking at a man in his sixties taking a nap.

"So, Doc, we've got a positive ID that this is Chuck Pfeiffer? I may have heard his name a million times but I've never seen him up close—"

"Lewellyn," said Osborne, admonishing her with raised eyebrows and forgetting that they both preferred he use her title when they were in public. "I've known the man since we were teenagers. Back when he was still living off his folks," he added with a sad smile.

"You know . . . " Lew paused as she glanced around the booth area that had been roped off for the Pfeiffer clan, "I guess I'm surprised that he didn't have security standing around."

"At most events he probably does," said Osborne, "but this tournament has always been about family: his family, all the families in Loon Lake. If there is one thing Chuck Pfeiffer did right, he refused to let his celebrity overshadow what the kids were doing today.

"Speaking of family, I arranged for his wife to wait for you in the bar. As you can imagine, she's stunned by what's happened, and once I saw that bullet wound, I made sure to get her out of here before she could trample on any evidence. The owners said she could use their office—I've asked Erin to stay with her."

Another siren sounded in the distance. "Oh, oh, that'll be the ambulance," said Lew. "I need to let the EMTs know they cannot enter the area. Doc, can you please call Dispatch and ask Marlaine to get in touch with Officer Martin?

"Tell her to let Todd know I need him out here ASAP to secure the entire Tall Pines property as a crime scene—including the dock, the boat landing, and the shoreline. And I need to tell the bar owners that no trash leaves here until we've had a chance to search it. I know it won't make them happy, but please let the owners know this bar is closed until the Wausau Crime Lab gives the okay."

"Got it," said Osborne, pulling out his cell phone.

With that Lew turned around to face the bystanders crowding in. "Please stand back—way back," she said, raising her voice as she approached the clusters of people who had been watching in silence since she arrived. Hands extended palms out, she herded the group in the direction of the parking lot.

When they refused to budge, she toughened her tone: "People, for those of you who don't know me, I am Lewellyn Ferris, the Loon Lake chief of police, and I'm sorry but I cannot have you standing here any longer. This is a crime scene. I want everyone back—way back. Behind the fence around the parking lot. Now."

Thinking she couldn't see them, two men in their twenties, beer cans in hand, ducked under the fence on the far side of the parking lot and circled back toward the awning and the silent figure in the chair. Twisting to face them, Lew called out, "Hey you two, if you don't get back to the parking lot ASAP, I'll arrest you for obstructing an investigation *and* violating the open container law."

The men, deer-in-the-headlight expressions on their faces, stopped right where they were, then turned and hustled back to the parking lot. "Thank you," said Lew.

She might not be the tallest police officer on the Loon Lake force, but Lewellyn Ferris had a heft to her shoulders and a torso strengthened by years of martial arts. When she spoke her voice was low, her approach direct, and her manner no-nonsense. Not even the drug-addled missed the message: This woman was in charge.

Lew had just finished updating the ambulance crew with the news that they wouldn't be needed until later when a van carrying the local station's television crew swung into view. A young woman scrambled out of the back of the van, video camera hoisted to one shoulder.

"Chief Ferris, we were just going down the road when we heard the news on our scanner," she called out, running toward Lew. "Is the victim really Chuck Pfeiffer? Who shot him? Have you arrested anyone?" Before Lew could answer, the girl hit the button on her camera.

"Sorry, miss. No interview. Please turn that camera off."

The reporter hesitated.

"You heard me. Care to spend the night in jail?"

The minute she spoke Lew berated herself for sounding so testy, but she had spent the entire afternoon in her office catching up on paperwork, a task guaranteed to put her in a bad mood. If that wasn't bad enough, she had been planning to enjoy a perfect summer evening with her fly rod and Dr. Paul Osborne until his call came in with the news of Chuck Pfeiffer's death. Afternoon wasted, evening ruined—but it wasn't the reporter's fault.

"Sorry," said the young woman, dropping the camera from her shoulder. "Just doing my job."

"Me too." Lew's tone softened. "Look, I just arrived here. My deputy, as well." She nodded toward Osborne who was heading in her direction having been able to reach Dispatch with all Lew's instructions. "Give me your card and I'll have someone call you the minute we have information we can share with the press."

The reporter hesitated. "Please, show some consideration," said Lew, hardening her voice. "Not even family members have been notified." That wasn't exactly true but it worked.

The reporter nodded and turned her camera on the crowd as she walked off in the direction of the parking lot.

"She may get better information than I have," said Osborne, watching the reporter who was now interviewing some of the people lingering in the parking lot.

"Let's start there then. Tell me what you know, Doc. Before Pecore gets here, and I expect him any minute now. Dispatch should have called him right when I headed out here."

Two seconds later her cell phone rang. "Pecore? What? You're breaking up. Where the hell are you?"

"Ontario," said a wheezy voice. "Canada. Can you hear me now?"

"Little better. What the hell?"

"Walleye fishin' up here one more day . . . with my brother-in-law."

"Nice of you to mention you were leaving town."

"C'mon, Ferris, I don't report to you." His words were belligerent and slurred.

"I'm talking professional courtesy, Pecore. You are the official coroner for Loon Lake and you have responsibilities—"

"I know, I know, but it's only a three-day trip."

"You think people only die on days you choose to be in town? Oh, forget it. You up there fishing walleyes with our good mayor, right?"

"You got it." He burped.

One of the frustrations of Lew's position as chief of police was working with Ed Pecore. A retired bar owner who was himself habitually overserved, Pecore had been appointed to his position shortly after his wife's sister's husband was elected mayor of Loon Lake.

More than once Lew had tried to have him relieved of his duties—due to incompetence (i.e., crucial evidence of a crime lost or damaged), absenteeism (due to hangovers), or bizarre behavior (allowing his golden retrievers in the morgue while conducting an exam on a defenseless deceased individual).

But once she discovered she could deputize Dr. Paul Osborne—a retired dentist with experience in dental forensics whom she met fly-fishing in a trout stream—she gave up trying to force out a man whose job security was ensured until the mayor and his wife divorced or died. Pecore didn't mind. So long as he got his salary, he was fine not showing up—he didn't really like dead bodies anyway.

"You might mention to your brother-in-law that Chuck Pfeiffer was murdered this afternoon."

"W-h-a-a-t—?"

With a satisfied grin, Lew clicked off her cell: Let those two walleye nuts stew on *that* for a while.

She beamed at Osborne. "Dr. Paul Osborne, you are officially requested to perform the duties of Loon Lake deputy coroner. Do you accept the appointment?"

Osborne returned the smile and nodded. Working with Loon Lake police chief Lewellyn Ferris might involve dead bodies and difficult people but he loved it. Or maybe it was all about her?

CHAPTER THREE

"Doc, let's take a minute to go back over what we know so far," said Lew, pulling a notepad from her back pocket.

"Well . . . on my end," said Osborne, sounding apologetic, "very little beyond the obvious cause of death and the fact it must have happened sometime after one thirty, which was about when Chuck stopped to chat with me for a few minutes, and three o'clock, which is when Erin and I were loading her SUV in the parking lot and we heard screaming. I ran over to see if there was a raccoon loose in the crowd or something more serious—like if someone needed a Heimlich maneuver.

"When I got here," said Osborne, waving one hand to indicate the area where he and Lew were standing, "I found Chuck right where he is, head tipped sideways so at first you couldn't see that hole in his head and his wife jumping up and down screaming. She didn't stop until I grabbed her by the shoulders and made her take a couple deep breaths.

"Once she got hold of herself, she told me he had been sitting like that for half an hour or more. She thought he had nodded off during the awards hullabaloo so she didn't realize anything was wrong until it was time for them to leave."

"Do we know if she touched him? Moved his body in any way?"

"No idea. The woman was on the verge of hysteria, which is why I asked Chuck's daughter-in-law, Charlotte, to take her over to the bar and get her to sit down. I also asked Erin to stay with the two of them until you could get here."

"Can't blame her for being upset," said Lew, "though she is now a very rich widow, isn't she." Osborne shot her a look.

"Just sayin'." Lew raised a hand palm out to deflect Osborne's critical eye. "So the daughter-in-law was there when . . . " She paused for confirmation.

"No," said Osborne. "Charlotte had been volunteering in one of the food stands and was helping to clean up when she heard the screaming. She arrived the same time I did."

"I see," said Lew, jotting down notes as he spoke. "Couple more questions before I go see Mrs. Pfeiffer. I mean, I guess there are two Mrs. Pfeiffers, aren't there." She sighed. "It'll be fun trying to keep that straight."

"Once you meet them you won't have a problem," said Osborne, itching to say more but that could wait.

Lew glanced up at him, "You wouldn't happen to know about how long the senior Pfeiffers have been married? Thirty, forty years maybe?"

While asking the question Lew had moved to one side and leaned forward to get a better view of the slack features of the man in the Adirondack chair. "He looks to be in his sixties, correct? With adult children, grandchildren . . . "

"One son from his first marriage. I've no idea how long he's been married to this woman—she's wife number three. He divorced the first one. That was Ginny. Number two committed suicide. Gail Murphy was her name. She was a patient of mine at the time."

Lew raised her eyebrows. "Suicide? How long ago was *that*?"

"Five years, maybe six. Mallory knows the story," said Osborne, mentioning the name of his oldest daughter. "She was a couple years behind Gail in school. Gail got an RN degree right after high school, which is how she met Chuck. He had a broken leg—fell over a log out deer hunting and she worked at the hospital where he was getting physical therapy. You can imagine the tasteless jokes—"

"I can only imagine," said Lew with a shake of her head. "I'll bet that McDonald's coffee crowd of yours went nuts."

"Made for a month of four-cup mornings. On the other hand, Gail was a very attractive young woman—"

"But if she was close in age to Mallory she must have been a lot younger?"

"Thirty years younger. *A-a-n-d* Chuck was having a midlife crisis."

Lew raised an eyebrow as she said, "Why do I think I've heard this story before?"

"Sad thing was Gail had a problem with alcohol and antidepressants."

"So she married a man likely to leave her a rich widow sooner rather than later but that wasn't enough?" asked Lew. "How'd she kill herself?"

"Pills. Could have been an accident I suppose, but I was told suicide by an old college friend of mine who's a psychiatrist up north. He was treating her for depression."

Osborne paused, thinking back over the incident years ago. Lew watched his face. "What? Are you thinking there might be a connection to the shooting today?"

"No," said Osborne, not sounding totally convinced. "I'm sure it was pills. And suicide. But I can check on that for you."

"And all this happened five years ago? Doc, I've been on the force for over six years so why is this news to me?" asked Lew. "Pecore is called in on suicides. Is this another death certificate he screwed up?"

"Oh, I doubt that, Lew. At the time Chuck and Gail were living up on the Cisco Chain where Chuck has—*had*—built a large lake home. So her death would have been recorded up there. Chuck managed to keep it out of the papers, which is another reason you would not have heard about it."

"That, plus I know how often my law enforcement colleagues in neighboring jurisdictions are generous with information." Lew's tone was dry.

A constant issue for the Loon Lake Police Department was the lack of shared information among police and sheriff departments, not to mention federal authorities, across northern Wisconsin and into Michigan. Too often major drug dealers were able to operate under the radar of law enforcement due to laziness within a department or mismanaged data sharing.

"Not sure that's a fair criticism. Do you alert Minocqua, Eagle River, Rhinelander, etc. to suicides here in Loon Lake?"

"As a matter of fact I do," said Lew. "I make sure death notices are posted whether they are natural, accidents, or otherwise. But you're right, Doc. They may have posted it and I didn't pay attention since there was no active investigation. Do I assume the victim still has a home up there?"

"No, he built a new place on the Wisconsin River just a few miles outside Rhinelander. And so far as I know that's where he's been living with this wife. Her name, by the way, is Rikki. Rikki Pfeiffer. Once known as Rosalyn. At least that's the name on her dental records from when she was a teenager." Osborne couldn't help the smirk that slipped in as he spoke.

"I hope Erin won't mind staying with the Pfeiffers for a few more minutes," said Lew while punching a number into her cell phone. "I have got to get one of the Wausau boys up here ASAP. They need to process this crime scene before the weather changes." She gave a nervous glance overhead. "I don't want to risk losing any evidence that may be on the ground or in the area. And we cannot move the body before then, either."

"Don't worry about Erin. She understands. She sent Mason and Cody home with friends so there's no rush as far as she's concerned," said Osborne as Lew's call went through.

Not only would his daughter understand the need for the delay, but Osborne knew he could count on her to be a keen observer of the two women waiting in the bar.

Besides raising his three grandchildren, Erin practiced law part-time and she was married to the county district attorney. She was the last person who would complain about sitting with a woman whose prominent husband had just been murdered. Her main concern might be the etiquette of the moment: It would not be polite to take notes while soothing the bereaved.

"Keep your fingers crossed I can reach Bruce Peters and not have to deal with Hector the director," said Lew with a grimace.

"Will do," said Osborne, folding his arms and making a mental note to call Ray and ask his neighbor to check on his dog. This was going to be a long evening, and Mike, his black lab, would need to be fed and his water dish checked.

Lew's call was answered and routed through to the forensic tech on call that Sunday afternoon. She held her breath, hoping she could avoid one of the more obnoxious individuals she was forced to deal with whenever the services of the Wausau Crime Lab were required. Loon Lake, like most Wisconsin small towns, depended on the crime labs based in larger cities.

Doug Jesperson, the recently retired director of the Wausau Crime Lab, was unilaterally despised across the Northwoods by women working in law enforcement for one simple reason: He never hesitated to let them know they could never be as smart or as strong as himself or any of the men they worked alongside.

Nor did it help that when he was around Lew, he stood too close and badgered her with one off-color joke after another. She could shut him down ("Doug, I don't listen to those kinds of jokes"), but she couldn't wipe the smarmy grin off his face. News of his retirement had made her day until she heard he planned to double-dip by subbing for crime lab staff on weekends and holidays.

Waiting for her call to be patched through, she counseled herself to stay calm and not give the creep the satisfaction of knowing he riled her.

"Yo, Chief Ferris, wind from the west means fishing the best. How the hell soon do you need me?"

"Oh, my gosh, is this Bruce Peters?"

"The one, the only—aren't you lucky?" Even over the phone she could hear her favorite forensic guru smile and see his bushy eyebrows bounce. Relieved at the possibility of getting the investigation underway with minimal hassles, Lew relaxed.

"And to whom do I owe this privilege?" she asked.

"My wife's sister had a baby so she's off to Appleton and I volunteered to relieve Jesperson. So, Chief, since the summer hasn't been too hot—think we can find time in the water? I'm still struggling with my casting. My line falls so short I'm ready to give up, buy a 3-weight, and fish midges."

"C'mon, Bruce, you'll never get a big brown on a fly rod with midges. Certainly not with a 3-weight. Might as well go back to fishing muskie with a spinning rod."

"I know, Chief, I know." His dejection came through the fiber optics cable loud and clear.

Lew couldn't help a sympathetic smile. For all his talent in the field of forensic science, Bruce was a burly guy who had a hard time not muscling the heck out of a weightless trout fly. But his failure was a blessing for Lew as she counted his hours in the trout stream with her as valuable as a private lesson with the famed Joan Wulff, who was legendary for her skill with a fly rod.

"Not to worry, kiddo—we can work on your casting. Once we find who shot Chuck Pfeiffer that is." Silence for a long moment.

"*The* Chuck Pfeiffer?" Bruce whistled. "Tell me more . . . "

After a brief update, Bruce said, "I can make the case that I need to be flown up ASAP and have my tech team drive our van. But I have one problem, Chief. We had a shooting during an attempted robbery at a pharmacy in Merrill and I'm short a photographer until tomorrow morning . . . "

"I'll get ahold of Ray Pradt. See you in what—half an hour or so? I'll have Marlaine make the usual arrangements for you at the Loon Lake Inn?"

"Good, but one more thing. Have you made sure the wife doesn't wash her hands? You said she touched the victim so—"

"Sorry, I didn't think of that. I'll get to her right now and hope she hasn't."

"Please, and if you can slip Tyvek bags on her hands that will help."

"I heard you mention Ray's name," said Osborne when she was off the phone. "I was about to call him and ask him to check on my dog—"

"Let me talk to him, will you? Bruce can't get a photographer up here until tomorrow. Ray has shot enough crime scenes for me that I know I can depend on him."

"Let's hope he's not off gallivanting with some attractive single mom he met today," said Osborne, punching in his neighbor's cell phone number. "Got voicemail," he said seconds later and looking up at Lew before leaving a message, "but there's a stretch on the way to his place and mine where neither of us get cell service."

"Damn. I could try that new photographer with the *Loon Lake News* but who knows if he's ever shot a crime scene. Ray knows the drill so well . . . "

"He'll call, Lew. This is about money."

CHAPTER FOUR

After retrieving two Tyvek hand preservation evidence bags from the trunk of her police cruiser, Lew motioned for Osborne to follow along as she headed up the gravel path to the entrance to the bar. They were twenty feet from the door when Erin stepped out and waved for them to walk back a short ways with her.

"Dad, Chief Ferris, I saw you coming and figured it would be okay for me to head home. That work for you, Chief?"

"By all means. And thank you for keeping tabs on these women," said Lew. "Gave me time to get our investigation underway."

"One last question, Erin," said Lew. "I don't suppose you have any idea about what time it might have been when Chuck Pfeiffer was shot?"

"Actually I do. I was going to tell you that as Dad and I were waiting for the awards ceremony to begin and some boys set off fireworks, I thought I heard a crack like a gunshot but Dad said it was more fireworks—kids had been fooling around with firecrackers all afternoon. But thinking back—that was one loud pop."

"And when was that?" Lew had her notebook out.

"I'd guess right around two thirty or a quarter to three? Maybe a few minutes earlier? Lots of people were here, some going down by the dock to watch the awards being handed out. Would you agree, Dad?" Osborne nodded. He'd forgotten about the pop.

"Erin's right about the pop, but I was hearing firecrackers all afternoon," said Osborne. "Some so loud I could swear they were *fireworks.*"

Before saying more, Erin glanced over her shoulder then turned so she had her back to the front of the tavern. Gesturing to Lew and Osborne to move closer as she spoke, she said in a low voice, "You'll find the two Pfeiffer ladies—Rikki and Charlotte—in the office, which is off to the right as you enter. They haven't said much to me or to each other. Let me put it this way: The room is chilly and . . . " she paused, raising her eyebrows to emphasize her words, "*it ain't the air conditioning.*"

With a wry grin she added, "Just so you know—when the senior Mrs. Pfeiffer saw you coming, she got very teary-eyed . . . " Erin's eyes signaled that the tears might be for their benefit.

"Noted," said Lew. "Thank you."

The room that Osborne and Lew walked into minutes later reflected the age of the old tavern. A battered metal desk took up the center of the small room, which had boxes of beer, liquor, and other supplies stacked ceiling-high along two walls. Osborne wasn't surprised since the tavern had been in existence since before his father had opened a dental practice in Loon Lake. Basements were crawl spaces or nonexistent in those days so space had to be an issue.

In a chair next to the desk sat the newly widowed Rikki Pfeiffer, one forearm resting on the edge of the desk while the other pressed a clump of Kleenex against both eyes. Lew gave a quick knock on the open door as she and Osborne entered the room. At the sound, Rikki sniffed loudly and shifted the Kleenex to her nose while keeping her eyes closed.

Osborne had to turn around to find Charlotte. The wife of Jerry Pfeiffer, Chuck's son from his first marriage, sat partially hidden in a chair pushed against the wall and not in full view until the door was closed. Later it struck Osborne she had been seated as far away as possible from the other woman.

Arms and legs crossed, right foot pumping up and down, Charlotte managed a nod in the direction of Lew and Osborne. The set of her jaw told Osborne she was less grief-stricken than her stepmother-in-law. Whatever color Charlotte's eyes might be under normal circumstances, at the moment they were pinpoints of black and flat as a snapping turtle's.

"Mrs. Pfeiffer," said Lew, addressing the widow in a kind voice, "before we talk I have to ask if you have washed your hands since touching your husband. I assume you may have touched him when he didn't respond—?"

"What?" The woman dropped the bunch of Kleenex from her face and stared at Lew. "What on earth? Why?"

"A forensic expert from the Wausau Crime Lab is on his way by helicopter. I expect him shortly and he'll need to check your hands for gunshot residue . . . "

"You think I shot my husband?" Her voice cracked.

"I didn't say that. But someone did and by touching your husband's body you may have picked up gunshot residue that can help with the evidence collection."

"If you're telling me I can't use the ladies' room and wash my hands . . . "

"Have you?"

"No, I have not, but that's disgusting."

"Disgusting or not, we need you to help with the investigation." Lew's tone had shifted from kind to firm.

Ignoring an expression of annoyance on Rikki Pfeiffer's face, Lew slipped first one then the other Tyvek bag over her hands, pulling drawstrings through string locks to secure them. As she did so, Osborne noticed the flow of tears had stopped.

"Good, that's done," said Lew, stepping back and straightening up. With that she introduced herself to each of the women. " . . . And this is Dr. Paul Osborne—"

"I know Dr. Osborne, he used to be my dentist," said Rikki.

"And mine," said Charlotte in a grunt from where she remained sitting against the far wall, foot still pumping. "But why is *he* here?"

With those words, Osborne recalled what a dour person Charlotte was and always had been. In her mid-forties and celery thin, Osborne once wondered if she might not be anorexic. "Oh, for heaven's sake, Paul," Mary Lee had said crossly when he had asked if she thought Charlotte might have a weight problem. "Charlotte Pfeiffer is a champion golfer. Golfs seven days a week when she can. And when she can't golf she gardens—she has a gorgeous garden. What would you expect?"

Osborne had opened and closed his mouth. He knew better than to argue that one. But he didn't buy Mary Lee's reasoning. Golfing, gardening, whatever: Charlotte Pfeiffer did not look well. Well? Hell, the woman looked like a witch. Even today in her pink button-down shirt over tan Bermuda shorts: classic golf attire.

But if Charlotte had the ability to hit a golf ball with unerring accuracy, when it came to basic human interactions she lacked both grace and a sense of humor. He had forgotten how hard it was to be around the woman, but then he hadn't seen her since shortly before he retired.

What he did remember was how she had taken to running ten to fifteen minutes late for her dental appointments. After the third time, Osborne had instructed his receptionist to say, "Mrs. Pfeiffer, you are so late, Dr. Osborne has rescheduled you for two weeks from now."

Upon hearing that, Charlotte had erupted with a stream of verbal abuse aimed at the poor receptionist until Osborne intervened. He suggested she choose another dentist.

That worked. Neither he nor the receptionist had to deal with Charlotte Pfeiffer again. Until today.

"Our coroner is out of the country at the moment," said Lew in answer to Charlotte's question. "Dr. Osborne fills in as deputy coroner when Mr. Pecore isn't available. So he'll be needing information from you," Lew had turned to Rikki as she spoke, "for the death certificate. Also, as deputy coroner, I'll be asking him to help me gather more details from each of you as we try to piece together what happened here this afternoon."

"You mean he'll *interrogate* us?" Charlotte's tone was demanding. "A *dentist*, for God's sake?"

"More like 'interview,'" said Lew, countering Charlotte's challenge with a smile. "As deputy coroner Dr. Osborne is often critical to our investigations as neither Loon Lake nor the county nor the Wausau Crime Lab can afford a full-time odontologist."

Seeing the confused looks on both women's faces, she said, "An odontologist is a health professional with expertise in dental forensics—the study of human remains and related matters. Fact is: teeth remain the gold standard for identifying a corpse.

"Dr. Osborne was trained in dental forensics during his years in the military. He continues that study by attending seminars offered by the Wisconsin Dental Society as well as specialized websites designed for medical examiners. I speak for both the Loon Lake Police Department and the Wausau Crime Lab when I say we are fortunate to have Dr. Osborne's expertise so close at hand.

"Any questions on that, ladies?"

Neither woman said a word. They seemed satisfied with her response, which was good as Lew had no intention of sharing the other reason she would ask Osborne to sit in on her "interviews" with the two women.

It wasn't until after Lew had deputized Osborne the first time that she realized what a valuable partner he could be during an interrogation. Her instinct was to listen for answers to her questions—while Osborne took a different approach. Years of observing patients with issues that may or may not be related to their dental health had taught him to listen between the lines. The spoken answer might not be the truest answer.

So it was that two years earlier Chief Lewellyn Ferris and Dr. Paul Osborne had discovered they made a good team when questioning key witnesses.

This had followed on the heels of meeting one another in the trout stream early one summer evening after Osborne had signed up to take lessons on casting a fly rod from a fellow named Lou. "Lou" turned out to be Lew and Osborne quickly became a struggling but determined student of fly-fishing.

They had known each other before this but from an arm's length—Lew was a patient of Osborne's since long before she entered law enforcement and long before he was widowed. That evening in the trout stream was serendipitous for both: not only was he encouraged to pursue a sport that had intrigued him, but she asked for and got his help working a current criminal case that required the skills of an odontologist.

Since then they had continued to collaborate on land, in water, and—though not as often as Osborne hoped—late into the evening.

CHAPTER FIVE

"My husband and I arrived here shortly after one," said Rikki Pfeiffer after Lew had asked her to give as many details of the afternoon's activities as she could recall. "We were running late because he had a morning meeting with my son, Bart, regarding management changes at the company that Chuck wants—"

"Damn you!" Charlotte jumped to her feet. "Chuck doesn't want any such thing. You—you're the one who wants that idiot kid of yours in charge," said Charlotte, her voice vibrating with anger. "Jerry and I know what you've been up to, you sneaky bitch—"

"Ladies, ladies—that's enough," said Lew, getting up from the folding chair where she had been sitting with her notepad braced on one knee. Raising her hands as if to quiet a crowd, she said, "I know you're both under a great deal of stress but this is not a time for confrontation." Ignoring Lew, Charlotte opened her mouth only to see Lew make a zipping motion across her lips. "I mean it, Charlotte."

Speaking slowly and deliberately, Lew said, "All I need to know right now—from each of you as witnesses—is *where* you were sitting, standing, or walking at approximately the time that Chuck Pfeiffer was shot. That is *all* the information I need. If other issues have a bearing on the case, we will deal with those later.

"So, Charlotte, if you will please sit down I'd like Rikki to go first." Lew turned to face the new widow. "Rikki, just tell me what you remember doing from the moment you arrived at the tournament with your husband—where you were standing or walking, anyone you may have spoken to, and what you were doing up to when you found . . . him."

Before Rikki had a chance to answer, Charlotte gave a loud snort and plunked herself down on her chair.

Osborne, watching from the folding chair he had set up near Lew's, wondered how much refereeing his good friend might be in for: Charlotte did not look like she planned to keep quiet for long. Just as Rikki started to answer Lew's questions, his cell phone rang. He glanced down to see Ray's name on the screen.

"Excuse me, Chief," he said, standing up phone in hand, "but the photographer we called is on the phone. I'll take the call outside." He hurried out of the tavern.

"Doc? I got your message and I'll head over shortly." Osborne could tell from the labored breathing that Ray was running. "Took care of your dog, my dogs, and I'm loading gear into the truck right now. Oh, and I grabbed that black bag from your office. Should be there in ten minutes.

"But, Doc . . . " Ray paused to take a deep breath, "were you kidding? Is it the Chuck Pfeiffer we know and love who's been shot? The same Chuck Pfeiffer who refuses to provide health benefits for his employees?" Ray was not a fan.

"Not kidding," said Osborne. "And it's going to be one long night over here. Bruce Peters is on his way but the Wausau boys are short on photographers. Busy weekend for the crime lab, which is why Lew was hoping you would have the time—"

"Hey, tell her not to worry. My guide bookings are down for the month—got nothing the next ten days so I can use the moola."

Osborne chuckled, "Are you ever not short of cash?"

Ray ignored his comment. "Doc, tell me where and when this happened so I am sure to bring everything I'll need. Was it inside the tavern? That SUV of theirs? Or outside somewhere?"

After Osborne had briefed him on Rikki finding her husband slumped in his chair under the awning and the fact that a bullet entering his skull behind the right ear appeared to be the cause of death, Ray asked, "Is there a lot of blood? Did the people who found the body make a mess of things before Lew could get there?"

"I was the second person to get close to the body after his wife found him and I made sure to keep people back," said Osborne. "No one has entered the Pfeiffer booth since without booties on. And there is so little blood that I told Lew he must have died within seconds of being shot. We'll wait for the pathologist to confirm that of course.

"Ray, all we know so far is that no family members were near when he was shot and no one remembers seeing any bystanders close by the booth, either. Not that there weren't a lot of people walking past but no one close enough to—"

"Sounds like a sniper."

"Oh, I doubt that. The man was sitting down. A sniper couldn't possibly have aimed through the crowd milling around the pavilion grounds. You were there. You saw how packed the place was. I'm not saying that's not possible, but I'll leave it to the pathologist who can say more once he or she sees the entrance wound."

"Hmm. Boy, if I were you, Doc, I'd tell Chief Ferris ASAP that I saw so many people taking photos and videos all afternoon that chances are good someone may have caught something on their phones or cameras. She needs to get hold of those. Maybe make that request on radio and TV right now? And before too many people leave the area."

"Good idea. I'll let her know that and see you when you get here."

Osborne clicked off his phone and ran back into the tavern office where Lew was jotting down notes as she spoke with Rikki Pfeiffer. "Sorry to interrupt," said Osborne, "but Ray has suggested we get a request out to the media that anyone taking photos or videos this afternoon should share them with the Loon Lake Police . . . ”

"Of course—why didn't I think of that?" Before he could finish, Lew was on her feet and heading for the door. She turned to the two women. "Ladies, please stay here. I'll be right back. Where's that television reporter?" she asked Osborne as she ran by. "Let's hope she's still in the parking lot."

She was. And by the time Lew had finished allowing the reporter to air the news of Chuck Pfeiffer's death "under questionable circumstances" along with the department's request for photos and videos, a beat-up blue pickup had pulled into the lot.

Sunlight flashed off a polished brass walleye that appeared to be leaping into the air from where it was glued onto the hood of the pickup. As the truck swung around to back into a spot near the fence separating the parking area from the grassy pavilion, Osborne spotted a brand-new white bumper sticker plastered across the tailgate. In neon green letters it read: *I have sex every day. Oops. No, I have dyslexia.* Ray Pradt had arrived.

Osborne watched as his neighbor unfolded his six-foot-six frame in sections from the front seat. "That man has more joints than a marionette puppet," Osborne's buddy, Don Jarvis, would mutter every time the McDonald's coffee crowd watched Ray enter and leave with his morning brew. Maybe old man Jarvis was jealous that Ray didn't even have to try to make an entrance. Came natural.

Today was no different. With his deep tan set off by crisp black fishing shorts and a white T-shirt emblazoned with the newest twist on his beloved mantra, *Excitement, Romance, and Live Bait—You Can Have It All Fishing With Ray*, he looked outfitted more for a day on the boat than an evening at a crime scene.

Later that evening when Bruce Peters teased him about his less than professional attire for the grisly job at hand, Ray gave him the dim eye and said: "Hey, bud, I was asked to get over here as soon as possible with my photography equipment—I wasn't asked to shave, shower, and have my hair done. So I hauled ass and this is what I happened to be wearing, okay? Before Doc called I'd spent my morning helping with kids and the fishing tournament. And I did a good job, too—not one of the little monsters got a fishhook in the ear."

Bruce's response? A big grin and a knowing shake of his head.

Appearances aside, Bruce did not hesitate to trust Ray's skill with the camera: He might be incorrigible, but he took damn good photos.

Lew knew that, too, just as she knew that Ray Pradt was more than just a guide to Loon Lake's most productive "honey holes" for trophy muskie and legal limit walleye. Even as she had learned to value his tracking skills in the woods and swamps that surrounded the lakes in the region, she had discovered that he brought the same disciplined and intuitive eye to shooting photos, whether the grim details of a crime scene or the poetic outdoor vistas he captured for the annual calendar put out by a local insurance agency.

So it was that over the last three years both Lew and Bruce had come to depend on the quality of Ray's work—plus he worked as fast or faster than the crime lab's own photo techs.

"Hey, Doc, here you go," said Ray as he handed him the black bag that held the paperwork and clipboard Osborne would need to complete Chuck Pfeiffer's death certificate. He turned to Lew: "You want Doc to point me in the right direction, Chief? I'd like to get started before the light changes." He glanced overhead where the summer sun was still high in the sky.

"That's great, Ray," said Lew, "but Bruce isn't here yet and even though Officer Martin has cordoned off the area we haven't begun processing the crime scene, so put on some booties, watch where you walk, and keep a close eye on the ground just in case you come across something that doesn't seem right. Know what I mean?"

"Yep, I do."

"Doc," said Lew, turning to Osborne, "after you get him started, will you meet me back up at the tavern, please? I want you there while I talk with Rikki and Charlotte."

"Whoa," said Ray, "you got both Pfeiffer women in the same room? Good luck with that."

Lew threw him a curious look. "Guess I'll have to ask you about that later."

"And I will be happy to share," said Ray. "Just so you know, in case Rikki sees me, I am *not* in her good graces."

"Really?" said Lew, raising an eyebrow. "Sounds like you and I definitely need to chat."

Minutes later as Ray trotted after Osborne, two cameras hanging from his neck and a duffel stuffed with more gear slung over one shoulder, he said, "Doc, I still cannot believe this. Chuck Pfeiffer murdered? How does that happen?"

At the sound of Ray's words, Osborne experienced a flash of memory from a conversation that took place at least thirty years ago at a time when Chuck's exploits in business and love had riveted most of Loon Lake. It happened over coffee at McDonald's, which had just opened in Loon Lake and during a time when Osborne was getting to know the men with whom he would be sharing that early morning delight—safe from the discord of family life and before the demands of the dental chair.

He couldn't remember who made the remark, which was after one of the fellas had updated everyone around the table on the latest of Chuck's bad behaviors. This one being his affair with the young wife of the son of one of Loon Lake's most prominent families— the same woman who would soon dump her husband to become Chuck's first wife. The speaker might be forgotten but his comment was memorable: "Why doesn't someone just shoot the guy?"

CHAPTER SIX

"Rikki's right about where she was before and after the awards ceremony," said Charlotte, her sullen expression making it clear she despised having to corroborate her stepmother-in-law's version of her arrival and activity during the final hours of the tournament. "Chuck insisted she be the one to give the winners their prizes this afternoon. He didn't want to do it. Because she had to be up on the stage she would not have gotten back to the Pfeiffer booth until after three.

"I know because," she rolled her eyes as she spoke, "I was watching the awards and I could *not* believe what she was wearing—"

"Thank you," said Lew, interrupting before Charlotte could finish her insult. "That information is just what I need for the moment, but I will be in touch with each of you later. I'm sure to have more questions for each of you as this investigation gets underway."

"Not together, I hope," said Rikki, tightening her lips as she got up from her chair and reached down to pick up a large white leather purse studded with black and silver metallic stars.

"No," said Lew, "Dr. Osborne and I will meet with each of you individually. I hope that will be first thing tomorrow morning unless something develops and we need to talk sooner."

She waved for Rikki to sit back down. "Sorry, Rikki, but Dr. Osborne needs a few more minutes of your time before you leave—for the death certificate. It won't take long."

"Certainly," said Rikki, sitting back down. Osborne waited for Lew and Charlotte to leave the small office before raising his pen over the document that needed to be completed. Since Rikki was busy looking for something in her purse, Osborne took a few minutes to study her closely. He could see why Chuck had been attracted to her.

Even though her face had fallen, whether from grief or exhaustion Osborne wasn't sure, she was easy to look at. She had classic Scandinavian features: wide cheekbones and the creamy skin, lightly freckled, of a natural blonde. Her generous lips parted easily over perfect white teeth, which Osborne could not help but notice had been recently and expensively capped. Her voice had a nasal but intimate timbre, and he knew, too, that on better days she had a lush, throaty laugh.

Years earlier, when Mary Lee was still alive, he had taken the family to the Loon Lake Pub for a Friday night fish fry where they had been seated at a table next to the Pfeiffers, who were entertaining friends he didn't recognize. But while the friends might have been strangers, Chuck's deep voice and Rikki's constant laughter were all too familiar.

The woman's laugh was so distinctive that his daughter, Mallory, the one who had inherited her mother's sharp tongue, had said after hearing her father comment on what a striking laugh Rikki had: "Jeez, Dad, trust me, she knows she has a great laugh. She laughs all the time for God's sake. Even when there's nothing to laugh about. It's her act, y'know?"

No, he hadn't known, but now he did. He chalked his ignorance up to one more thing he didn't understand about women.

That conversation had taken place long after "Rosalyn Thornton" had morphed into "Rikki Nickel." The surname change occurred after her first marriage to a real estate developer from Wausau, Jim Nickel, who was the father of her son, Bart. To lure investors that poor guy had falsified his financial statements only to find himself parked in a federal prison camp for white-collar bad actors. It took less than six months for Rikki to divorce him.

She wasn't single for long. Slim-hipped with a narrow waist and bountiful breasts, she was a magnet for men—and she knew it. She had sorted through her suitors with care until she had found just the right one, the one who could afford her tastes, the one who was burdened with an emotionally disturbed young wife and was ready to appreciate a woman with a throaty, sexy, happy laugh: Chuck Pfeiffer.

But what had befuddled Osborne then—and still did—was the woman's lack of class in presenting herself: She didn't leave much to the imagination. For all the money Chuck Pfeiffer had (not to mention her first husband pre-prison camp), Rikki dressed, as Mallory put it with succinct distaste, "like a hooker."

Even today Osborne couldn't help but be aware that she was wearing shorts shorter than any his granddaughters wore. Her blouse, though currently buttoned three buttons higher than two hours earlier when she had discovered her husband's body, made it obvious there was little if any upholstery underneath.

Osborne's questions took less than five minutes. "I have no idea," Rikki said in answer to each whether it was Chuck's date of birth or his full legal name. "I'll have to call our family lawyer tonight and get you those details. I'm sorry, Dr. Osborne. I've never had to pay much attention. Chuck handled all our personal business."

"Well, one last question then," Osborne said. "To the best of your knowledge did Chuck have more than one child? Is Jerry Pfeiffer his only child?"

"Yes," said Rikki. A look crossed her face as if she realized what that meant. "Dr. Osborne," she said, her voice tightening, "that means I'm the one who gets all his money, doesn't it?"

"Now that is a question you have to ask your lawyer," said Osborne. "I can't imagine Chuck doesn't have a will. I'm sure his son Jerry will share in the estate—"

"But Chuck was rewriting his will. See, he and Jerry . . . well," she hesitated and Osborne waited, silent, watching her face. Had she said too much? "Um . . . he was not going to leave Jerry and Charlotte . . . um, what he had planned to.

"So I get it . . . all, I guess. Maybe," she raised her eyes to Osborne's and they were frightened eyes, "maybe I'm next?" Her hands shook as she reached down for the purse she had set down by her feet. "I'm calling my son to pick me up. Then I'll call the lawyer for that information you need."

———————

Trudging down to the pavilion area where he had spotted Lew, Osborne heard a gruff voice call his name. He turned toward the parking lot. An old man sitting on a bright yellow three-wheeled motorcycle waved for him to come over.

"Sorry, Harvey," said Osborne, walking toward the parking lot. "I'm busy right now. Can we chat some other time?"

He was peering into a face so ravaged by years of sun and wind that the old man looked like a potato left too long in the field. But it was a familiar face. Harvey was a patient he had inherited from his father. The guy had to be eighty-five at least but tough enough still to be riding a motorcycle, even if it was a trike. And he had most of his teeth—two were implants but the rest were functioning.

"No, came by to give you a warning, Doc." The old man was not smiling.

"A warning? About what for heaven's sake?"

"One of those grandkids of yours. The girl. You know, the tall one."

"You mean Beth? She's fifteen."

"She's got a boyfriend—"

"Oh, I don't know about that—" said Osborne cutting him off, worried the old guy had jumped to some disturbing conclusions.

"I was down by the river back of the Loon Lake Market a half-hour ago and one of the sheriff's guys was arresting her and the boy. Somethin' to do with drugs. Thought you should know."

Osborne was stunned. "Are you sure it was Beth? Beth Amundson?"

"I've known your family for years, Doc. Yeah. The girl. The tall one."

"Okay. I'll see what it's all about. Thanks, Harvey."

The old man had started to wheel his bike around to leave the parking lot when Osborne asked, "How did you know where to find me?"

"I didn't. I was jes' goin' by and saw you walk outta the bar. My place is right down the road from here."

"Oh. Well, thanks, Harvey." Osborne paused on his way to the pavilion to check his phone for messages but there were none. He trotted along the path by the dock to catch up with Lew.

"Do you have anything on the scanner about a drug bust down behind the Loon Lake Market?" he asked.

"No, why?" She gave him a puzzled look. "All I've had in the last half-hour is some nutcase calling for an ambulance to come and get him because 'he can't stop drinking' and, Doc, I am not making that up." She started to smile but when she saw the worry in his eyes, she stopped. "Let me check with the sheriff's department . . . "

"I see," she said to the dispatch operator. "Thank you."

Turning to Osborne, Lew pursed her lips and said, "It's kids and marijuana but no arrests. At least not yet. Parents have just been called to come meet with the sheriff's deputies who picked the kids up. And, yes, Beth is one of them, Doc. Sounds like they'll be cited but no arrests. They've been trying to reach Erin and Mark but they aren't answering their cell phones or the home landline. They're keeping her in custody until they can reach them."

"I'm sure the family is out on Mark's pontoon with their phones off or no cell service. I better go into town, Lew. Sorry."

"Of course, Doc. Call me when you know more, please?" She grabbed his arm as he started to leave. "Don't jump to conclusions. There is so much weed in town these days that your granddaughter may be an innocent bystander . . . "

"Or not," said Osborne. "Good try, Lewellyn, but I've raised two daughters who sure as hell didn't get through their teens without trying . . . " He was so upset he couldn't finish his sentence.

CHAPTER SEVEN

Slumped back against the long wooden bench with her arms crossed tight to keep from shivering in the air-conditioned room where the sheriff's deputy had told her to wait, Beth stole a look at the girl sitting at the other end of the bench. Dressed in a short black skirt, sleeveless black blouse, and lace-up black leather boots, she had scarlet and black tattoos running up both arms and down both legs. Beth wondered what artwork might be hiding *under* the clothes.

A silver ring hung from her nose and long silver earrings dangled from her ears. She had short, spiky black hair that looked dyed and silver studs outlined her ear lobes. Sitting with one leg crossed over the other, the girl made no effort to hide that she was bored out of her mind.

Acutely aware of what she herself must look like with her wheat-colored hair pulled back in a ponytail, no make-up, and wearing white tennis shorts, a white T-shirt, white tennis shoes, and nary a body piercing in sight—Beth felt like a little kid in the presence of a witch goddess. She was afraid to say a word. Having never seen the girl before, Beth assumed she had to be from the cities—Minneapolis or St. Paul. Maybe Madison. Places where the action is.

"Can't even have a goddamn cigarette?" the girl demanded of the quiet room. She turned to Beth, eyes glowing behind dark rims of eyeliner. "What you in here for? Go through a stop sign on your way to church?"

"No," said Beth, belligerence surging. She was her mother's daughter after all. She didn't have to let herself be intimidated. She made an instant decision to exaggerate what had put her in this awful spot. "Caught dealing."

"Oh yeah?" The girl's eyes brightened. "Like . . . oxy? Meth? What?"

"Just weed," said Beth offhandedly, working hard to sound like she considered marijuana small-time stuff.

"You don't look like a dealer," said the girl, a challenge in her voice.

"That's the secret," said Beth. "I teach little kids tennis. No one would expect me—"

"Then how'd you get caught?" The girl looked at Beth with a mix of curiosity and admiration.

"One of my friends has a big mouth—"

"Man, do I know that story." The girl slid down the bench to sit closer to Beth. "You at the high school here in Loon Lake? Ever meet a guy named Pete?"

"Yeah, I go to Loon Lake High," said Beth, "but the only Pete I know is Peter Dondoneau who's on the tennis team."

"God, no, the game Pete plays is craps." The girl grinned. "But he is cool."

"Your boyfriend?"

"Yeah, I guess. He got me all these tattoos." She held out her arms.

"Nice," said Beth. "What are you in here for?"

The girl grimaced. "They got me for prescription drugs with no prescription. Pete'll get me out, though. He knows the system. It'll all be hunky-dory." She sounded confident that a few hours from now life would be good.

Beth nodded. She knew better than to mention that her father was the district attorney. He knows the system, that's for sure. Her problem? Nothing in her life was going to be "hunky-dory." Not for months.

Tears pressed against her eyelids. Truth was she had not been dealing. Truth was she had never smoked marijuana or even wanted to. Truth was she was sure she would lose her summer job, her cell phone, and she would be grounded for the summer.

"What's your name?" The girl's question interrupted Beth's thoughts.

"Oh, I'm Beth Amundson. What's yours?"

"Wendy. Wendy Stevenson. We should get together sometime. I know Pete would like to meet you. He's always looking for people on the inside at Loon Lake High. Hey, do you know Jake Cook?"

"Not really," said Beth, starting to wonder if this new friendship was a good idea. The boy Wendy had mentioned was one of the stoners that Beth and her friends avoided. As the boy rarely came to class, avoiding him was not difficult.

The door opened and a woman in uniform beckoned to Wendy. "This way, miss, I'm a deputy sheriff and I want you to follow me, please."

"About time," said Wendy, getting to her feet. "Maybe now I can have a ciggie?" She pointed a finger in Beth's direction. "I'll be telling Pete about you. See ya 'round, girlfriend."

Twenty minutes later the deputy returned to the room. "You're next, young lady," said the woman. "Come this way, please." Her noncommittal tone held a hint of kindness that had been missing in her directions to Wendy. Following the deputy down a long hallway to a small office, Beth wondered how much worse the day could get.

"Have a seat, Beth," said Sheriff Peterson as she walked into the room. "I know you were caught in a difficult situation and I'm sure your parents will have plenty to say to you. No arrest but you will be cited for being in the presence of an illegal drug sale. Your father can explain what that means exactly." He gave her a sympathetic glance.

A knock at the door prompted the sheriff to say, "Dr. Osborne? Come in."

Osborne walked into the room and took the chair next to Beth. "I heard you were here, sweetheart," he said. "The sheriff's department couldn't reach your parents. They took Mason and Cody for a ride on the pontoon to celebrate Mason's award and must be somewhere the cell service is bad. I'll be taking you home."

"Not quite yet, though, Doc," said the sheriff. "I need to ask Beth a few questions first." The phone on his desk rang and he picked it up. He listened then gave Osborne and Beth a quick look. "Sorry, have to take this. I'll be right back," he said and left the room.

"Beth," said Osborne, his voice somber as he turned in his chair to face his oldest grandchild, "I need you to tell me what happened. How did you get here?"

Dropping her face into her hands, Beth started to cry.

"Ssshh, it'll be okay," said her grandfather, leaning to reach over and rub between her shoulder blades. "This is not the end of the world."

Beth sniffed hard and wiped at her eyes. "Umm, Gramps, you know my friend Kevin, right?"

Osborne nodded. "Good kid. I know his folks."

"Well, his cousin, Philip, is visiting from Colorado and he brought some marijuana with him. It's legal there, y'know."

Eyes hopeful, Beth waited for assurance that her grandfather knew the legality of marijuana was a matter of dispute. Osborne nodded, "I do know that, Beth. And it is legal in a number of other states—but not in Wisconsin."

"So Kevin and my friends, Larry and Colin, were going to buy some from him. I went along 'cause Kev and I are, I mean we *were*, going to play tennis after." She wiped at her face again.

"We all met in the parking lot out back of the market 'cause Kev's been working there this summer and he was getting off at four.

I was just standing there waiting for Kev. That's all." She couldn't help a quick sob.

"So you did not buy any?"

"No. And I didn't smoke any, either."

Hmm, thought Osborne, *not yet anyway.* He knew better than to expect any of his grandchildren not to experiment eventually. But he believed Beth.

"It isn't the smoking that I worry about, Beth. It's the people you find yourself being around. That's why I want you to be careful. And it happens to all of us. For my generation it's been alcohol. Perfectly *legal* but something that can easily get out of control . . . " He paused.

His granddaughter had averted her eyes and he realized she must have heard her parents talking. Talking about Osborne and his own descent into an abyss of heavy drinking after Mary Lee's death when her bronchitis had turned deadly in the middle of a winter blizzard. That had been a bad, bad year.

Only now could he look back and see that even though he and Mary Lee had drifted into parallel and not always friendly lives that the patterns of those lives had been his moorings. When she was gone, his world was shaken. And bottle in hand he had swooned. Only a courageous intervention undertaken by his two daughters had helped him shake the miserable choice he'd made. Months in rehab had followed—and saved his life.

"You know what happened to me, don't you?" he asked. She was old enough to know the truth however ashamed he might feel. Beth raised her eyes to meet his.

"Yes, but I'm—I'm just trying to tell you I didn't smoke."

"Sorry, maybe I'm overreacting here," said Osborne with a weak smile. "It's because I love you and I worry. Can't help it," he smiled again. "I'm your grandfather."

"I know, Gramps," she said, patting his hand. "It's okay. I know you're just trying to help." Her understanding took him aback: Which of them was the older and wiser?

At the sound of footsteps coming down the hall, Osborne said in a low tone, "Okay, Beth, here is what I want you to do and this is very important. When Sheriff Peterson asks why you were in the parking lot with the boys, all you say is that you were meeting Kevin before going up to the high school to play tennis. That's all. You do not mention any names: not his cousin, not Larry, and not Colin.

"You take responsibility for being there but you do not—to use an old-fashioned word—*tattle* on anyone. If he asks who else was there, simply say you can't answer that. You must tell your parents everything, of course. Then let your father decide what you can and cannot say legally. But right now that is all you say. Understood?"

Beth nodded and whispered, "Yes."

"Have you already told anyone about the other boys being there?" asked Osborne.

"No. Right away the deputy put me in a separate car and no one has asked me anything yet."

"Good. Did you see the boys pay for the marijuana?"

"No. I had just got there and Kevin and I were waiting for his cousin and the others to arrive."

"I wonder how the sheriff's department knew about the drug deal?" Osborne asked.

Beth shrugged. "Kevin told a bunch of us about his cousin having weed to sell. Maybe someone told their parents?"

Or someone who felt left out of Kevin's circle of friends, thought Osborne, remembering the emotional turmoil of his own adolescence. Given the Colorado connection, Kevin probably didn't think twice before bragging, much less to whom he was entrusting his exciting information. He might be a good kid but he is a teenager. Osborne knew from experience there is no one as stupid as a bright fifteen-year-old who thinks he or she knows it all. Logical consequences? Never enters their heads.

Beth followed Osborne's instructions and within twenty minutes she was released to his custody with a citation. Leaving the sheriff's department, Osborne saw two more sets of parents, grim-faced, approaching the building: Larry's and Colin's.

Opening his car door for a chastened Beth to climb in he thought, *Curious how summer evenings can take a left turn.* His cell phone rang. It was Erin.

"Jeez Louise, Dad—what on earth is going on?"

CHAPTER EIGHT

At seven thirty that evening Osborne pulled into his driveway hungry and tired but relieved that Beth was home with her parents after following his instructions to incriminate no one other than herself and her tennis partner. Whether she had known about the pending purchase of marijuana was not Osborne's overriding worry. Her parents could deal with that issue.

His concern was elsewhere. Since childhood, his father had ingrained in him the importance of not blaming others for your mistakes, and if there was any life principle he was determined to pass on to his children and grandchildren it was that: Take responsibility for your mistakes and keep your mouth shut.

He continued to mull over Beth's predicament as he let Mike out to chase a chipmunk, then canvassed the refrigerator in hopes of a surprise treat. A quick call to Lew as he drove home had assured him he wasn't needed back at Tall Pines and the crime scene. But what he did need to do was get in touch with Rikki Pfeiffer for the details necessary to complete her husband's death certificate. Deciding that had priority over hunger, he closed the refrigerator door and punched in the phone number she'd given him.

"Yes, Dr. Osborne," said Rikki, answering his call immediately. "I reached our lawyer and I think he's given me everything you need. He also mentioned that Chuck had not signed his new will, which means—"

"We can discuss that in the morning," said Osborne, stopping her before she could get started. "Chief Ferris will want to know the details." What he didn't add was that Lew would want that interrogation videotaped. Faces and voices can offer more insight than words, particularly words heard on a cell phone. Or words repeated so often they lose their impact.

"Do you know when and where I can tell the funeral home to pick . . . um . . . my husband up?" She had carefully avoided saying the word "body" and he sympathized. He knew from the hours following Mary Lee's death how long it takes for the finality of death to become real.

"We won't know that for another day, maybe longer, Rikki," said Osborne. "There has to be an autopsy, which may take place in Wausau. I'm sure Chief Ferris will be in touch with you as soon as she knows."

Five minutes later, having completed the death certificate, Osborne set the paperwork aside to be delivered in the morning. After wolfing down a liver sausage sandwich and some stale potato chips, he headed to the lower level of the house and the project he had set himself for the summer: turning the bedroom once used by his youngest daughter into a workshop for a certain someone whom he hoped to persuade to spend more time at his place.

Convinced after three tries that Lew would never agree to marriage, he now hoped that if she had her own space in his home where she could relax with her favorite hobby—tying trout flies—that she might spend four nights a week at his house instead of just two. He was planning to surprise her with the finished workshop on her birthday, which was two weeks away.

Over the last month he had been able to carve out an hour every few evenings to work on the space. So far he had been able to take up the carpeting, refinish the wood floors, and paint the walls a soft cream that would lighten the room. Tonight he planned to tackle the window trim. Once that was done he could look into ordering equipment and supplies. He was loosening the lid on a quart of paint when he heard a noise overhead.

"Who's there?" he called, walking over to the stairway to look up.

"It's me, Doc," said Lew. "Bruce is with me. We need to talk to you." Osborne spun around to close the door on his surprise and headed up the stairs, anxious to reach the living room before Lew could come looking for him.

"I thought the two of you would be working most of the night," said Osborne as he walked toward them.

"Funny thing," said Bruce, rocking back on his heels and thrusting his hands into his pockets with a self-satisfied grin. "The minute our good governor heard who the victim was he found what sounds like a hundred thousand dollars somewhere to beef up our investigation.

"First he wanted to send in the FBI. Once I persuaded him that was not necessary—at least not until we know more—I was able to arrange for two forensic techs to drive over from Green Bay. They got here an hour ago and they'll work the crime scene till dark. The three of us will be back there first thing in the morning but I need some history on the Pfeiffer family first. For context, know what I mean?"

Osborne knew exactly what he meant. Could Chuck Pfeiffer's killer be among his nearest and dearest?

"Just look at that lake," said Bruce as he walked onto the screened-in porch that ran the length of Osborne's home and overlooked Loon Lake. The three of them paused to admire the early evening glory: the water shimmering as if copper coins had been spilled among the ripples streaming toward shore.

"Bruce has been asking me about the Pfeiffer family and I figured you'd be as good a person to start with as anyone," said Lew, settling onto the porch swing, "or if not, you'd know to whom we should talk. Right, Bruce?"

"Chief's right," said Bruce as he pulled over a wicker armchair. "This was no random killing. Someone had it in for the guy. Someone skilled with a handgun. You rarely see a person killed with just one bullet. And the stats tell us most murder victims die at the hand of someone they know."

"Not sure if I can tell you everything you need but I can get you started with some background that might help," said Osborne. "And given Chuck's questionable actions toward some folks over the years, you may be looking at a long list. I am a good place to start, by the way, since years ago Chuck Pfeiffer was a patient of my father's . . . until Dad fired him."

The two sets of eyebrows facing Osborne rose in unison.

"Now, Dad wasn't the only person who wanted nothing to do with the guy. Every one of the six men in Dad's deer shack—with the exception of one and that was Chuck's father—voted to tell Chuck he was persona non grata there, too. But this was years ago—a good forty years—take or leave a year or two."

The porch swing gave a soft creak while out on the lake the sun had departed, leaving behind pools of pale rose laced with periwinkle blue. Osborne settled back in his chair, ready to reminisce.

"The Pfeiffer story starts with the McClellan brothers, whose ancestor, Herman, ran a trading post on land bordering the Wisconsin River and on which was founded the town of Loon Lake. Over the years the trading post became McClellan's Sport Shop run by Bob and Joe McClellan, old Herman's great-grandsons.

"I know this because whenever I was home from boarding school, my dad and I would stop in there first thing and there was a plaque on the wall behind the cash register honoring Herman and his trading post."

"So you didn't go to school in Loon Lake, Doc?" asked Bruce, surprised. "Guess I never think of people living in a small town like this sending kids off to boarding school. I take it your family was well-to-do?"

"Not at all," said Osborne. "We weren't poor but my father wasn't rich. What happened was my mother died when I was six and my father sent me off to Campion, a Jesuit boarding school down in Prairie du Chien. But all my summers were spent here with my dad, who was also a dentist—and a fanatic muskie fisherman." He grinned. "In case you've ever wondered why I've fished muskie all these years."

"Summer mornings Dad and I would have our oatmeal and start the day talking lures and spinning rods and whatever might be new on the shelf at McClellan's Sport Shop. Later, while my dad was busy in the dental office, I was allowed to walk to McClellan's by myself.

"I loved the shop: the smell of earthworms and minnows, the racks of rods and reels, and this big box of ice that was kept out front on the sidewalk to display trophy fish customers might have caught that morning. What a place it was—the aisles so crammed with hunting and fishing gear, you had to walk sideways. Paradise for a kid who fished."

"Paradise for a dentist who fished sounds like to me," chuckled Bruce.

"You bet," said Osborne. "My dad liked to say he practiced dentistry for one reason only: so he could afford to fish.

"I would wander up and down the aisles listening to customers chewing the fat with Joe, who was never without a Camel hanging from his lip. Joe manned the cash register and he was brilliant when it came to advising on what lures were catching the big girls or showing a kid like me how to untangle a bird's nest in my fishing line. In those days I wasn't the only boy in Loon Lake who thought of old Joe as my favorite uncle."

"And where was this sport shop located?" asked Lew. "I grew up in Tomahawk and my grandfather owned a sporting goods store, too, so we never came to Loon Lake in those days."

"McClellan's used to be where the Fish Hook Tap is now—just off Main Street. So Joe was the one who kept the shop stocked to overflowing and he never married. Bob handled the books. He married Harriet and they had one child, a son named Martin who took over running the store after his uncle Joe died of lung cancer in his early fifties. Martin's father, Bob, had already died of a heart attack at the age of forty-eight.

"Martin had just turned twenty-two when he took over the store. He was a couple years older than me but in those days I was in dental school so I never really knew Martin. Meanwhile, Chuck Pfeiffer's family had moved to Loon Lake a few years earlier when his father was hired to manage the paper mill.

"Martin and Chuck became close friends in high school and they did some hunting and fishing together. Right about that time my father and his hunting buddies invited Chuck's dad—and Chuck—to join the deer shack. Martin had been hunting with the men since before his father died.

"By the time Martin took over McClellan's Sport Shop he had married Ginny Nelson, whom he had begun dating in high school. The shop was thriving in those early days and I'm told the ladies in town considered Martin quite the catch. Ginny was petite, dark-haired, and—as my daughters might say 'cute.' She had been captain of the cheerleaders and prom queen with Martin as her prom king. 'Star-crossed from birth those two' was what Dolores, my dad's housekeeper, once told me.

"People who knew the family expected Ginny to get pregnant right after the wedding and raise lots of little McClellans. Made sense: so long as there were fish in the lake and deer in the woods what could possibly go wrong for Martin and Ginny McClellan?"

"I can tell from the sound of your voice *that* didn't happen," said Bruce who had been leaning forward, elbows on his knees and chin cupped in one hand, listening to Osborne.

"N-o-o-o, it did not. A year or so after his marriage to Ginny, Martin ran into financial difficulties. Word among my dad's friends was that he lacked his uncle's knack for stocking quality fishing and hunting gear, nor was he the raconteur that old Joe had been. People stopped hanging out and spending half their paychecks in the shop. Pretty soon the trophy fish icebox disappeared, too.

"Martin wasn't happy running the operation, either. He told my father that it was his mother who insisted he keep it going long after he knew he could have sold at a nice profit, but Harriet wouldn't let that happen. She has always been one fierce cookie. It didn't take long for the shop to be foreclosed on: Martin McClellan went bankrupt.

"I have to qualify what I'm going to tell you next because the rest of the story is what I heard from my late wife who played bridge with Martin's mother, Harriet."

"So this won't be Ginny's version?" asked Lew with a knowing smile.

"No, it won't and I can't vouch for the accuracy of the details, either."

"All right, we'll consider the source," said Lew, giving the porch swing a push. "Go on."

"At the same time that Martin's shop was tanking his buddy, Chuck Pfeiffer, was doing great business-wise. Chuck's old man had set him up with three gas stations that had bait shops attached: a winning combo in those days.

"Didn't take long for Chuck to do well enough to buy himself a fancy speedboat, perfect for waterskiing on the big lakes. One afternoon Martin decided to drop by the boat unannounced for a chat with his pal only to find Ginny on board drunk and wearing a bikini that Martin told his mother later he had never seen.

"Martin went ballistic and was reaching for her arm to yank her off the boat when Chuck gunned the outboard motor. Martin catapulted off the back of the boat into the water. His right leg got caught in the propeller and was badly mangled. When I heard the story later, I was surprised he hadn't bled to death. But they got help from some people on shore who saw the accident and called for an ambulance. Martin survived but the marriage didn't.

"Shortly after the accident McClellan's Sport Shop was put up for auction. The straw buyers turned out to have been hired by Chuck and his father, and the rest of that story is an astounding retail success. With his father's financing behind him, Chuck was able to enlarge the existing store at the same time that he got into discount merchandising of hunting and fishing gear. In less than ten years he had opened twenty-eight other locations statewide, and I believe there are over seventy Pfeiffer's Fishing, Golf, and Shooting Sports sporting goods stores today.

"Oh, and he married Ginny McClellan. That's when the men in the hunting shack had had it—they booted him out. My father was disgusted, too, and told Chuck and his father to find themselves a new dentist."

"What happened to Martin?" asked Bruce, throwing a quick look at Lew. "Maybe we should be looking him up?"

"Martin remarried and took a job selling cars. His leg was so damaged he never hunted or fished again and the poor guy died in his early forties—a blood clot in his bad leg traveled to his lung or his heart. I'm not sure. Afraid you'll find him in St. Mary's Cemetery. His wife is buried next to him. She had breast cancer and died several years later."

"Sad story," said Lew. "I take it Chuck is no longer married to Martin's ex? The woman I saw today is way too young to be her . . ."

"No, but Chuck and Ginny had one son together and that is Jerry Pfeiffer. You met his wife, Charlotte."

"Yes, I did," said Lew with a roll of her eyes. "This helps to explain why I sensed an animosity between those two women when I was interviewing them. Charlotte especially. She seemed so angry. I didn't realize it was directed at Rikki."

At the sound of a rapping on his kitchen door, Osborne glanced down at his watch as he said, "Who on earth can that be at this hour?" Getting to his feet, he called out, "Who's there?"

"Me, Dad," said Erin, striding through the living room toward the porch. "With Mark. He needs to know more about the Pfeiffer case—"

"Before I get slammed with the press in the morning," said Mark with a grimace as he walked in behind his wife. "First questions will be about my daughter—then it'll be all about Pfeiffer. Chief Ferris, I'm hoping you and I could handle a press conference together?"

"Very good idea," said Lew. "Let's plan to meet for coffee around seven?"

"Sorry to interrupt, but is Beth doing okay?" asked Osborne.

"As good as you could hope," said Mark. "I explained to her that it's important for all of us that she be cited like any teenager would be in that situation. Fair is fair even if your father is the DA. But Erin and I believe her when she says she wasn't there to buy weed."

"She told me she's worried she'll lose that summer job . . ."

"I called her coach and explained what happened. He wasn't happy but he's shorthanded so he's willing to let her keep helping as his assistant on the courts on the condition she goes straight home afterwards—no hanging out with friends. Her mother and I agreed especially as she's grounded for two weeks anyway. Long enough to make her think twice before she ends up in a dicey situation again."

"Welcome to the world of raising a teenager," said Lew.

"It's never easy, is it," said Erin, giving Lew a sympathetic hug as she sat down on the swing beside her. Everyone on the porch, including Bruce, knew that Lew had lost her only son at the age of seventeen in a bar fight.

"Drugs, alcohol—it's bound to be something," said Mark. "I'd like to think we might luck out with our kids but who knows. They have to learn somehow." He shrugged and turned to Lew. "So what is the latest on the Pfeiffer shooting?"

Osborne got up from his chair and turned to Lew and Bruce, "Why don't you bring Mark up to date while I get all of us some snacks." He left the room.

"Not much yet to answer your question, Mark," said Lew. "Bruce has a team working the crime scene as we speak though I'm sure they've given up for the night."

"No," said Erin, "we just drove by Tall Pines and the site is all lit up."

"Good," said Bruce, "no rain is forecast but you never know in this part of the woods. The more work we can get done before weather intervenes, the better."

Minutes later, after describing the crime scene and what little information she and Osborne had been able to glean from the widow, Lew said, "I'm afraid that is all we know so far. Doc was telling us that Charlotte is married to Chuck's son from his first marriage. I understand that Wife Number One is still alive. Is that correct?"

"I believe so," said Mark, turning to his wife. "Erin, do you know where Ginny Pfeiffer lives these days?" Mark asked.

"Florida," said Erin. "She's been there for years."

"Did you ever know her?" asked Lew.

"I saw her a couple times as a kid but all I really know is the gossip. I remember hearing my mother describe Ginny as 'a bitch of a wife who got dumped like she deserved.'

"But . . . " Erin looked around to be sure her father was not in hearing distance before saying, "my mother was never kind about any woman outside her bridge club—and she was merciless when it came to Ginny."

"Did Mary Lee know Ginny well?" asked Lew.

"Didn't matter. My mother was in awe of Harriet McClellan, Martin's mother. And Harriet, in my humble opinion, was and is one of the most unpleasant women in Loon Lake—a vicious gossip. At the risk of sounding like an ungrateful child, which I am, I have to say my mother was not kind, either."

No one said a word for a long moment. "I'm my father's child," said Erin. "People think children don't judge their parents or that the parents are always right. I knew at age sixteen that my mother was unfair to many, many people, including my dad."

Mark reached over to touch his wife's hand. "I've had good therapy," she said with a quiet laugh. "Mark's right. I need to shut up. Well . . . one more thing. Dad has never said a word against my mom—not to me anyway—but, boy, she and Harriet could really tear people down. For those two a woman like Ginny Pfeiffer was raw meat."

Lew smiled. "Are you implying the Loon Lake Ladies Bridge Club might have lined up to do Chuck Pfeiffer in?"

"Of course not. But I do know that people don't forget."

CHAPTER NINE

Beth hummed as she walked along the road leading to the tennis courts at the senior high. The morning was crisp and sunny with a hint of the hot summer afternoon to come. She still couldn't believe her good luck.

When her dad had called her tennis coach the night before, she had held her breath, certain the coach would say he didn't want her teaching the kids anymore. But he didn't. Maybe the fact that he has two sons in college made him more than a little understanding. He and her dad laid out a few rules for her to follow, but they said she could keep her job as the coach's assistant so long as she didn't screw up.

She made up her mind to find extra things to do around the courts, which was why she was showing up early this morning. First thing she could do was sweep all the pinecones off before Coach Moore even arrived. *That's the ticket,* she thought happily, humming again.

Though the tennis courts were nearly two miles from her house, she didn't mind the walk. It got her up and finished with breakfast before Mason and Cody could bug her, and if the weather was lousy one morning no big deal. The tennis clinic would be canceled and she could sleep in. Plus her folks appreciated that she didn't insist on a ride. Her dad had left the house at six thirty that morning and her mom was on the phone with one of her law clients.

Beth stepped off the curb to cross the street and was starting up the final quarter of a mile to the courts when she became aware of a Jeep Wrangler slowing as it drove by her. A man with dark hair pulled into a ponytail stared out the window on the driver's side as he drove past. *Mind your own business,* she thought to herself, annoyed. *Haven't you seen a girl in tennis shorts before?*

Bounding onto the tennis courts a few minutes later, she was pleased to see that she was the first to arrive. She grabbed the court broom and got busy.

Two hours later, after walking the last ten-year-old to his mom's car, Beth hurried back to the courts to gather up her racquet and backpack. Slinging the backpack over her right shoulder, she gave a quick skip as she headed for the street. Thoughts of what she would fix herself for lunch kept her feet moving fast.

Beth was nearing the courthouse green, which was a block from her home, when she noticed a Jeep Wrangler parked on the side street near the intersection where she crossed kitty-corner to walk through the park around the courthouse. The car was too far away for her to see who was driving.

Bounding up the front porch steps to her home, she heard a passing car give a quick beep. One of her friends? She turned in time to see the Jeep Wrangler slow down as it went by. A girl with short, black spiky hair waved to her from the passenger side: Wendy Stevenson, her new best friend. Driving was the guy with a ponytail who had driven by her early that morning.

"Something wrong, hon?" asked her mother as she walked into the kitchen.

"No, I'm fine." But she didn't like the feeling in the pit of her stomach.

CHAPTER TEN

Lew pulled her cruiser into the parking lot of the Loon Lake Police Department shortly after six A.M. She was anxious to see the report from Bruce's forensic team plus the photos from Ray. A late call to Ray had been reassuring, as he said that he had made sure to shoot alongside the two forensic techs from Green Bay until they had completed processing the crime scene.

"Chief," he had said, sounding tired, which was no surprise since she was calling at ten thirty that night, "the three of us worked like dogs until the sun set. I'll be sending everything I got in as JPEGs and PDFs. Think that'll do it?"

"I hope so," said Lew. "Can't thank you enough, Ray. See you in the morning? Bruce and I are sitting down to go over the early reports at six thirty. I know that's early but—"

"I'll be there. Heading out at five for bluegills if you want to join me."

"Thanks but have to pass."

Hurrying through the front entrance to the department, she was stopped by the raised hand of Marlaine who was working Dispatch that morning. "'Morning, Chief," said the woman who had been working Dispatch for over twenty years now and was the unofficial boss of the department. "Dani needs to see you. She's in your office and she's having a nervous breakdown."

"Another one?" asked Lew and she opened the locked door leading to the department offices. "I thought she had one last week. After that bad date she met on Match.com."

Marlaine smiled and adjusted her headset. "This is serious. I'm keeping a phone line open for her to make a call once she has your approval."

"Ouch, this does sound serious."

Dani Wright was in charge of IT for the Loon Lake Police. She had been hired full-time a month earlier after eighteen months as an intern while completing a degree in law enforcement through the University of Wisconsin system.

And she was a surprising hire from the first. Lew had stumbled on her when she was enrolled at the local tech college studying to become a cosmetologist. Dani had been working part-time in student services where her supervisors had discovered she had an uncanny skill with computers and database searches. So when a criminal case involving the school's network needed someone with IT skills, it was Dani who proved valuable in helping with the online investigation.

After leaning on the young woman to help the Loon Lake Police with another investigation requiring advanced computer skills, Lew had been able to persuade her to switch from hair, nails, and make-up to focusing on criminal investigations, which might not be as glamour-driven as salon work but potentially better paying.

Flattered by the recognition of her talent with keyboards and cell phones—plus her innate understanding of the Internet with its hazards and possibilities—Dani had opted for the career change. Plus it got her into the Wisconsin retirement system, which brought her parents enormous relief.

The only issue faced by Loon Lake police chief Lewellyn Ferris was Dani's appearance: She wanted to keep her long, meticulously cut, curled, and colored (some days streaked purple) hair. And she did not want to wear a uniform.

"Style counts for me," she had argued. "I work better when I feel good and I feel good when I know I look drop-dead."

Drop-dead? Lew considered Dani's interpretation of that term, but okay. "If it takes being 'drop-dead' to get you to our computer terminal, then that is okay with me," she had said, naming a salary that would allow as much cutting, curling, and coloring as the girl could manage without having her hair fall out.

So how critical could an issue in the life of Dani Wright be on a day when the entire state of Wisconsin would be looking for the answer to who killed their wealthiest entrepreneur?

"My server crashed at four o'clock this morning," said Dani as Lew walked into her office. "You told me to expect a *few* photos and videos—not *thousands*. And who knows how many are trying to load now. I mean, Chief, can't we just use surveillance video from that tavern?"

"What makes you think the Tall Pines Tavern, which is over a hundred years old, would have surveillance cameras all over the place? They aren't McDonald's. Anyway, the only town around here that has cameras like that is Rhinelander. This is Loon Lake. I'm lucky I have cameras watching who comes in our front door."

"Guess I watch too much *CSI*," said Dani. "I've called our tech support but right now I can't even get e-mail."

"Hold on," said Lew. "Let me make a call."

Dani leaned back in her chair, crossing one yellow capri-clad leg over the other and letting her sandaled foot swing while Lew punched in Bruce's cell number.

"Good morning, Mr. Peters," said Lew when Bruce picked up, his voice sleepy. "Any chance our good governor would mind if we spent some of the money for the Pfeiffer murder investigation on a new server?" She listened, then said, "I am not kidding. We have been overwhelmed with people sending in digital photos and videos from the tournament. You know my IT person, Dani—she doesn't expect us to be able to access those for hours, maybe days . . . " Lew winked at Dani who winked back.

"Thank you. I'll have her make the call ASAP. Good, see you in half an hour." She turned to Dani, "Okay. Call your tech support people and order us a new server—one that will work for us for another five years if possible."

"Really? That will be expensive."

"Dani, the governor has authorized the Wausau Crime Lab to spend whatever is needed to solve this case. Chuck Pfeiffer was one of his largest donors over the years and he's committed to finding the person who killed him. Look at it this way: The Loon Lake Youth Fishing Tournament aside, Chuck Pfeiffer is still doing good things for the Northwoods." She couldn't resist a big grin.

"This is so cool," said Dani, jumping to her feet. "I'll bet you I'll have a new server up and running by lunchtime."

"I alerted one of our pathologists of the governor's special interest in this case and that the victim was being rushed down to Wausau for an autopsy," Bruce was saying an hour later as he and Lew met with Mark Amundson before the press conference, which was scheduled for eight that morning. "He went to the autopsy room last evening and was able to send me preliminary findings this morning."

"That's fast work," said Mark. "I hope you told him that Chief Ferris and I appreciate it. Any surprises?"

"Yes," said Bruce, "and I suggest we keep it confidential until we know more. But first the basics: The victim died almost instantly from a single bullet to the brain stem. Evidence indicates a hard contact wound angled to hit the brain stem. The shooter knew what they were aiming for."

"Do we know what type of gun was used?" asked Lew as she wrote down Bruce's information.

"A handgun," said Bruce, "a .357 Magnum revolver. The bullet was lodged in the victim's head so if we're lucky enough to find the gun, ballistics can match it to the bullet."

Lew glanced up in surprise. "Who uses a .357 anymore? He's sure it wasn't a Sig Sauer P226 9 mm? Those are much more common these days." Bruce shrugged.

"Is that the surprise?" asked Mark.

"No. As they were prepping the corpse for the autopsy they found a plug of spittle in the victim's hair."

"Spit or phlegm?" asked Lew.

"Good question," said Bruce. "Spit, I believe. We'll know soon. Now whether the shooter spit before shooting? Or another individual walking by might have spit? The victim was sitting along the open side of that booth so it would have been very easy for someone going by to just lean over and—"

"Spit." Mark finished the sentence.

"Wait a minute," said Lew, "and we'll know more later today when Dani is able to pull up the photos and videos people have been sending us, but think how many people spit when they're talking. If you consider the volume of noise with music blasting over the loudspeakers, kids setting off firecrackers—hell, anybody trying to say hello to the man might spit without meaning to."

"True," said Bruce. "But enough was found that one of my colleagues has sent it out for DNA testing."

"Think the governor can ratchet up the time frame on how long it'll take for us to get results?" asked Lew.

"We'll see," said Bruce. "I've got the request in."

Lew looked down at her watch. "The TV van has been out front for an hour now and we've got three reporters waiting. One drove up from Madison at the crack of dawn this morning. Are we ready, guys?" Mark and Bruce nodded as they got up from their chairs. "Good. Showtime."

Osborne, sitting beside Lew in the department's conference room, watched in silence and scribbled notes off and on as she interviewed Charlotte Pfeiffer. Lew had deliberately avoided meeting with her in the casual setting of her office or the severe interior of one of the interrogation rooms. But if she had hoped the business-like setting would calm the woman she was wrong.

Charlotte was so wired she hummed. At least that was how she struck Osborne with her lips pressed tight and her hands trembling even as she tried to keep them clutched in her lap. "You have to understand," she said, sputtering, "Jerry was in line to become CEO of the Pfeiffer Corporation until Rikki forced that son of hers on Chuck—which made no sense whatsoever."

"When did Jerry discover that Bart might be promoted?"

"Chuck told him two weeks ago."

"How did Jerry take that?"

Charlotte paused then said, "That he was being pushed aside? He should have been angry. *I* was angry."

"Of course," said Lew, "but what was your husband's thinking about the change in management."

Charlotte looked away in exasperation. "I have no idea. Sometimes Jerry doesn't make sense. My point is: *he can run that company*. He has worked there since he was a teenager and it isn't that difficult. I could run it."

I'm sure you think you can, thought Osborne, before saying, "If Jerry wasn't angry at 'being pushed aside' as you said, why are you so upset?"

"Oh, he always takes the easy way out," said Charlotte. The disgust in her voice told Osborne everything he needed to know about the marriage.

Realizing what she had said, Charlotte waved a hand to backpedal. "Wait, I didn't mean that the way it sounded. What I meant to say was he didn't want to upset his father. Jerry loves Chuck. He always thinks of Chuck first: What does *Chuck* need? How can he help *Chuck?*"

"Let's assume that Chuck is still alive and he promotes Bart to CEO. What does that mean for Jerry?" asked Lew.

"He would handle special projects and work part-time."

"And get paid part-time?"

"Oh, no. He was to get full salary . . . unless Bart changed that, too."

"But now that Chuck is gone, what will happen?"

"Jerry takes over, of course," said Charlotte, sitting back with a satisfied expression on her tight features. Osborne couldn't help thinking she was one of the most unattractive women he had ever encountered. It wasn't that her skin was mottled from teenage acne, or that her eyes appeared permanently narrowed in suspicion—it was her judgmental attitude. He couldn't imagine being married to a woman like that.

Osborne caught himself. Wait, Mary Lee had grown into the same kind of person as the thirty years of their marriage went by: dismissive of his decision to practice dentistry in small-town Loon Lake instead of Milwaukee where "you could have made much more money, Paul"; dismissive of his fishing buddies "who wear those baggy old pants and smell of swamp—keep them out of my house"; dismissive of his relationship with his daughter, Erin, as she was growing up—"for heaven's sake, Paul, she has a ballet class today. I don't care if she wants to go fishing with you. Ballet is very important."

Without a doubt Charlotte and Mary Lee shared a singular attribute: a lack of kindness including a lack of consideration for another person's point of view. Poor Jerry. Osborne suspected that, like him, Jerry gave up arguing long ago. Maybe even gave up saying much of anything to his wife. If so, how would she know what he was thinking?

"Now that your husband is boss, what will that mean for Bart?" asked Lew. "Oh, and before I forget to ask, where was your husband yesterday afternoon between one and three?"

"Fishing. Told me he was going to fish Horsehead."

"Who with?" asked Lew as she looked down to jot a note on the legal pad in front of her.

"Alone. He always goes alone."

"Well . . . " said Lew glancing up, "we will need a witness for where Jerry was yesterday. We know where you were but we need witnesses for the whereabouts of all family members. That includes Bart, too. You can understand why."

Charlotte gave an impatient sigh. "I am the witness. I watched him leave our driveway with his fishing boat on the trailer."

"We need someone who saw him at Horsehead Lake between one and three P.M. yesterday afternoon, Charlotte," said Lew, her voice firm. "Where is your husband right now because I would like to speak with him as soon as possible?"

"He's in his office of course. Someone has to run the business," said Charlotte, making no effort to hide her irritation. "If you had mentioned this earlier, I could've had him come in with me."

"If I had wanted both of you here, I would have said so."

Silence. A sullen look on her face, Charlotte reached into her purse and pulled out her cell phone.

"If you're trying to reach your husband, you'll have better reception outside," said Lew. "And you have my cell number?" Charlotte nodded. "He can call me direct when he has a moment and we'll arrange a time to talk. Thank you, Charlotte." Lew gave her a gracious smile.

Once Charlotte had left the room, Lew turned to Osborne. "What do you think?"

"I think Jerry Pfeiffer keeps to himself," said Osborne. "I doubt that woman has a clue as to what her husband really thinks or plans or even who the guy really is."

CHAPTER ELEVEN

"Hey . . . " yipped Ray as he unfolded, section by section, his six feet six inches through the front door leading to the hall, which housed the offices of the Loon Lake Police Department, at the same time as Charlotte was heading in the opposite direction, "Charley Pfeiffer . . . how . . . the heck . . . " he pointed an index finger at her nose, "ya doin'?"

Ray had a habit of breaking up his "commentary" (as he liked to call it) with pregnant pauses that forced listeners to suspend whatever momentum they thought they had in life until he finished his sentence. This could be entertaining or supremely irritating.

"None of your goddamn business, and stop calling me 'Charley,'" said Charlotte, eyes focused straight ahead to ignore Ray as she stomped past. Osborne, observing the two from where he stood in the doorway to Lew's office, grinned as he beckoned to Ray.

"'*Charley*? Where did that come from?" he asked, stepping aside so Ray could enter the office.

"She used to babysit for us when we were kids," said Ray. "We all called her 'Charley.' Or . . . when she couldn't hear us . . . 'Sourpuss.'"

"So she's always been . . . unpleasant?"

"Long as I've known her. N-o-o-o sense of humor." A glint entered Ray's eye. "Which only makes it that much more fun to torture the woman."

"And I'm sure you do," said Lew with a chortle from where she was sitting at her desk.

"Got your message on the server crashing so I brought this along," said Ray, reaching into the backpack he had slung over one shoulder. He pulled out his laptop computer.

"Fire that sucker up, Ray, and show us what you got." After a long, silent viewing of the photos on Ray's laptop computer, she sat back in her chair. Thinking, she swiveled the chair from side to side. "So no surprises really," she said at last. "Am I right or did I miss something?"

"Nothing unusual that I could see—or that showed up in either black and white or color," said Ray. "I took photos of the entire Pfeiffer booth from top to bottom, the chair where Pfeiffer died, and I made sure to shoot around the area as well. I checked with the two forensics guys working the scene with Bruce to make sure I didn't miss anything. You got it all." He sat back in his chair. "Need anything more from me?"

"Not at the moment," said Lew.

"Wait, I have a suggestion," said Osborne. "Since Ray knows more people in this town—maybe *around* this town—than I do. Or you, Chief. And we know that Dani's going to have hundreds of photos and videos that people took yesterday—"

"That many?" asked Ray, surprised.

"Enough to crash her server," said Lew. "Doc makes a good point. I should have you look at those, too. See if you recognize anyone. Or see things going on in the background when someone is taking video of their kids. The more eyes we have on those pictures, the better."

She didn't add what she was thinking: The vision and intuition that made Ray an excellent tracker over field and swamp and through dense, dark cedar forests might pick up details in the shadow and light of a digital image missed by an untrained viewer.

"Do you have any record of threats that your husband may have received in recent weeks?" Osborne asked of Rikki Pfeiffer. Having known the woman from the days when she was "Rosalyn," and known Chuck since before he was a twenty-two-year-old homewrecker, Lew had asked Osborne to take the lead on questioning the widow.

"Oh, yeah," said Rikki, "this one old man sent threats to Chuck all the time. He used to leave nasty notes at our front gate. Even in winter when the envelopes got all soggy from the snow. He was always threatening to kill Chuck."

"How do you know it was an old man?" asked Osborne. "Anyone in particular?"

"Oh, yes—it was Gail Murphy's father. Gail was Chuck's wife before me—the one who killed herself."

"Do you mean Clarence Murphy?"

"Yeah, Clarence. That old creep."

"Rikki, Clarence Murphy died over a year ago."

"Really? Well, that explains why we haven't gotten any in a while," she said, her voice flat.

Osborne was quiet. He wasn't sure how to respond. He wanted to say that Clarence Murphy was not an "old creep." He was a retired pediatrician whose wife had died years ago in a car accident on an ice-covered bridge. The death of his only child, which he swore was the result of Chuck's philandering and lack of sympathy for his young wife's despair, had devastated the old man. Osborne could only imagine the man's fury.

"Gail died under very sad circumstances," he said, recalling the conversation with his friend, the psychiatrist who had treated her for depression and alcoholism before her suicide. "I'm not surprised her father sent angry notes. Better than showing up with a shotgun, wouldn't you say?"

"Her killing herself was not Chuck's fault."

Are you so sure about that? Osborne wanted to ask. The rumor had been that Chuck had taken up with Rikki long before his second wife's death. Oh well, no point in opening that line of inquiry.

"Other threats?" he asked.

"Not unless you count Jerry being such an ass. You know he threatened to sue his dad if he promoted Bart."

"I didn't know that. How far has that gone?"

"Oh, he—I mean Jerry—backed down." She gave a harsh laugh. "Of course he *would*. He is such a wuss. And you would think he could see the writing on the wall for Christ's sake."

"How so? I thought Jerry was in line to become CEO, too. Most people in Loon Lake assumed—"

"Well, they can stop assuming. Let's be real, Dr. Osborne. Jerry Pfeiffer has never been out of Loon Lake. He has a two-year degree from a tech college and he's married to that . . . that . . . oh, forget her. She's a whole 'nother story.

"My son went to Princeton and has an MBA from the University of Chicago and he learned the nitty-gritty of doing business from one very smart man—his father. *Bart knows how to run a billion-dollar company.* Jerry has no clue, plus he's slimy as a leech and twice as spineless. Chuck could see that." Her voice had risen while she talked and she finished with her chin thrust high though Osborne suspected she knew she had said too much.

Lew couldn't keep quiet any longer. "When you mention Bart's father are you referring to your ex-husband who went to prison?"

"Yes, I am. But Jim is brilliant. He has an amazing head for business and he's taught Bart everything—made sure he went to the right schools, gave him the best advice for getting ahead."

"Excuse me for bringing this up again, but isn't your former husband in prison for fraud?" Osborne was befuddled by her rationale.

"No. Jimmy was released from prison three months ago and he's living in a halfway house here in Loon Lake. But only for another couple months." Her voice had softened as she spoke her ex-husband's nickname. "And for the record he was framed. The financial records he was accused of forging? Baloney—he kept excellent records like all real estate developers do. Jim's problem was he was too successful and someone with more political clout was able to nail him on some teensy-weensy error in the financials and get their grubby hands on land that belonged to us. You know, Chuck agreed with me that Jim had done nothing wrong. It was a-a-l-l politics."

"He did five years, isn't that right?" asked Osborne. He knew the case well as his son-in-law had been the prosecuting attorney.

"Yes, but he went to a white-collar camp with some other guys who got railroaded. He'll be back on his feet in no time. Just wait and see," said Rikki sitting back with her arms crossed and a sandaled foot pumping.

"If he's such a smart guy, why did you divorce him?" asked Lew. "Five years isn't that long a sentence."

"He lost all our money."

Lew waited for Rikki to say more and when she didn't, Lew said, "Are you in touch today?"

"Of course. Bart is his son." She paused then added, "Chuck understood."

He did? Osborne wanted to ask. Didn't sound like the Chuck he knew.

———◆———

"I would imagine she owns enough of the Pfeiffer Corporation now to boot Jerry out even if he is an heir to some of Chuck's fortune," said Osborne as he and Lew compared notes after Rikki had left the building.

"So Jim Nickel is back in town and his former wife—now a very wealthy widow—is convinced her 'Jimmy' was framed." Eyebrows arched, Lew gazed at Osborne with a slight smile. "How many times have I heard that one?"

"And 'brilliant,'" said Osborne. "Don't forget 'brilliant.'"

CHAPTER TWELVE

The new server went online at one fifteen that afternoon. Dani watched, eyes widening, as the photos and videos flooded in: The television and radio requests had been heard. Three hundred seventy-two photos and eighty-nine videos later, Dani exhaled.

"How on earth do I do this, Chief Ferris?" asked Dani. "I mean, I'm not sure what I'm looking for—there is so much. No wonder the old server crashed."

Standing behind her, alongside Lew and Osborne, was Bruce. All three had their eyes glued to the screen. "I have a suggestion," said Bruce. "Given we're trying to determine who was in the crowd yesterday, why don't you put head shots or photos focused on just one or two people in one folder? But photos of the crowd and those that show people in the background can go in a different folder, which is the one we'll want to look at." He caught Lew's eye. "Does that make sense?"

"Yes," said Lew, "but what is more important is any photo or video that shows the Pfeiffer family's booth and any people standing in or near it. That's the key: Who was close enough to Chuck Pfeiffer to place a gun at his head?"

"So you want the Pfeiffer booth?" asked Dani, sounding dubious. "Not sure how I'll know what's what, Chief."

"Dani, start by taking a close look at the photos that Ray shot at the crime scene yesterday. Once you do that you'll be able to identify the Pfeiffer booth easily."

"It's the only one *not* selling hot dogs," said Bruce drily.

"Really?" Dani was looking a little less rattled.

"Yes," said Lew. "Once you get started it'll all make sense."

"But what if I miss something?"

"Dani, all I am asking you to do is sort through and get rid of any photos or videos focused on one or two individuals—like a child and a mother. If other people are shown in the pictures, leave those for us to review. Doc, Ray, Bruce, and myself will take it from there. Got it?"

"Oh, okay. I can try," said Dani, "but I need you guys to leave the room so I can concentrate." She gave a heavy sigh.

As Osborne, Lew, and Bruce walked into Lew's office, a call from an unfamiliar number came in on her cell phone. She waved Osborne and Bruce over to the small conference table in the corner as she answered. "Hello?"

"Chief Ferris, this is Jerry Pfeiffer. Charlotte said you wanted to speak with me. I'm in town at the moment. Just had a haircut. Would this be a good time? I can be there in five minutes . . . "

"That would be helpful," said Lew. "I'll have the front desk send you back to my office." Shutting off her phone, Lew joined the two men sitting across the room. "Bruce, would you please excuse Doc and myself? That was Jerry Pfeiffer, Chuck's son who wasn't at the tournament yesterday. We need to know where he was during those hours."

"Hey, I understand," said Bruce. "I'll check with Dani. She knows me and maybe if there's just one of us she won't mind my watching her work. I am very interested in seeing what people have sent in because right now—unless you know more than I do, Chief—we've got zilch to work on."

—◆—

Jerry Pfeiffer was a tall, lanky man who walked with a permanent hunch. Even his facial features, asymmetrical with a receding chin, seemed to be folding in on themselves. If anything, he looked like a man who didn't want to be noticed. And that was in contrast to his father who had the build and confidence of a linebacker and a face that thrust itself forward even when not invited.

From what little Osborne had glimpsed in passing of Rikki's son, Bart, the latter resembled his stepfather more than the man's own son—both in stature and a natural presence. He could see why Chuck had favored Bart: He carried himself with authority.

Meanwhile, every time Osborne had seen Jerry Pfeiffer over the years he had had to resist the urge to tell him to stand up straight and stick his chin out. Back when Osborne was still practicing, Jerry had been a regular patient, though he had never needed anything but a cleaning by Osborne's hygienist, which meant Osborne rarely had occasion to speak with him at length. Nor had he wanted to. The guy was so nondescript that when he left the room even the memory of him was gone.

Also, he and Osborne were too far apart in age to have hunted or fished together, but Brian, the young boy whom Chuck had treated so poorly when he didn't finish first in the tournament, was Jerry's son. Osborne decided to say something good about the kid right away in hopes it would get back to him and help the little guy feel better about that day.

"Thank you for coming by, Jerry," said Lew as Jerry walked into her office. "You know Dr. Osborne? He's been deputized to help out with our investigation."

"Really, Dr. Osborne?" asked Jerry, shaking their hands. "I thought you were retired." He sat down in the chair next to Osborne.

"Yes and no," said Osborne. "I'm retired from my dental practice but my background in dental forensics has put me right smack in Chief Ferris's sights," said Osborne with a laugh. "Given Loon Lake has such a small police force, I try to help out when I can. Before I forget, Jerry, I want to compliment your son on his fishing in the tournament. He may not have finished first, but I watched his casting and he'll do well. I'm sure he'll land a fifty-incher one of these days."

"Brian was pretty disappointed, but it was my fault," said Jerry. "I told him to use a spider jig and it didn't work very well."

"You did?" asked Lew. "That's for bass."

"I know," said Jerry, shaking his head with a wry smile, "but they had those kids fishing that weed bed in front of Miller's Resort and that spider has a great helicopter action that punches right through weeds. And how many muskie do you reckon know the difference?

"But . . . " he grimaced, "it didn't work. Brian was bummed. We're selling a lot of those spider jigs in all our shops these days, though."

"Jerry," said Lew, sounding anxious to change the subject. "Where were you yesterday afternoon between one and three?"

Jerry looked stunned at the question. His mouth opened and shut but he said nothing.

"No offense, Jerry," said Lew, "but this is a question I am putting to all family members."

"I see. Um, I was out on Horsehead Lake fishing for bluegills. Go almost every Saturday. Sounds selfish I know—I should've been there for Brian. It's just . . . well, it's my one escape from the business." Jerry smiled. "Keeps me sane." Osborne saw his right upper lip twitch.

"I can understand that," said Lew. "And who would have been fishing with you?"

The question seemed to confuse the man. "Or have seen you put in and take out? I assume you use the public landing out there?"

Again, the twitch. "Humm, gee . . . I can't think of anyone who might have seen me. At least no one I know."

Lew and Osborne sat quiet, waiting. Jerry cleared his throat and pursed his lips.

"I'm sorry, Jerry," said Lew, "but if you don't have a witness for where you were during those hours, I will have to consider you a suspect in the death of your father."

"You can't be serious." Jerry cleared his throat again and shifted in his chair while staring down at the floor. The room was quiet.

"Okay," said Jerry after a long pause, still staring down, "do you know Gloria Barnes?"

"No . . . I don't think so," said Osborne. Lew shook her head negatively, too.

"She works for us in accounting . . . "

"And?" asked Lew in a calm voice.

"I was with Gloria yesterday. All afternoon. She's my . . . " He didn't finish his sentence and he didn't look up. "Do you have to tell . . . Charlotte?"

"No, we don't," said Lew. "But I could certainly use a better witness than a girlfriend who might be willing to cover for you."

"Could one of her neighbors be a witness? They see my boat and trailer in her drive."

"Worth a try," said Lew. "Name and phone number?"

Lew had Osborne make the phone call as the neighbor Jerry mentioned was a retired worker from the paper mill and someone Osborne knew from when he had treated the man after he'd taken a hockey puck in the mouth.

"Am I going to get that poor guy in trouble?" asked the gruff voice on the speaker phone.

"Quite the opposite, Frank," said Osborne. "If you can vouch for his being next door yesterday afternoon, you'll be keeping him *out* of a great deal of trouble."

"He was next door alright. He's there every Saturday so far's I know. Lucky sonofabitch." He snorted.

"But did you actually see him coming or going?"

"Yes, I did. My wife and I were spreading mink manure in the garden when he drove up. I was worried Gloria might complain so I asked him to tell her the smell would go away in a couple days. That stuff stinks, y'know."

———◆———

Jerry paused in the doorway and turned to say, "Charlotte told me that you asked that anyone who had photos or videos from yesterday's tournament to e-mail them to the Loon Lake Police. Is that right?"

"Yes, we're hoping that someone may have inadvertently taken a picture of whoever it was that shot your father. We've received quite a few and several of us—myself and Dr. Osborne included—will be hoping to see something that'll help with this investigation," said Lew.

"I think we may have something that will be of great help," said Jerry. "Our events manager, Carlyn Shaw, had a video crew working in the booth and during the awards ceremony yesterday. I'm going to have her give you a call right away."

He left, closing the door quietly behind him while Lew and Osborne sat with their mouths open.

CHAPTER THIRTEEN

Lew's phone rang ten minutes after Jerry had walked out. "Chief Ferris? This is Carlyn Shaw from Pfeiffer's Fishing, Golf, and—"

"Yes, Carlyn, Jerry Pfeiffer said you would be calling," Lew interrupted. "He said you may have some video that can help us?"

"Let me tell you what we have and I'll be happy to send you a link to the material. It isn't edited yet but that may be what you need anyway. First, I'd like you to know that the two people who set up and manned the Pfeiffer booth were from my staff. They were helping the family all afternoon until the awards ceremony when they were down on the dock giving Mrs. Pfeiffer a hand with the awards."

"You mean Rikki Pfeiffer?" asked Osborne.

"Yes, and after the awards were taken care of they came back to the booth where they thought Mr. Pfeiffer was taking a nap—which he has been known to do before—so they packed up their things and left. They were supposed to return later to take down the booth but I think you know that we've been told not to touch anything until the Wausau Crime Lab gives us the okay."

"Correct," said Lew. "But what is this video that you referred to?"

"I planned for us to make a video of the Youth Fishing Tournament to be shown at the company's annual meeting in September. I don't know if you're aware but our little Loon Lake event's been written up in national sports pages like the *New York*

Times and *USA Today*. Gosh, even *CBS Sunday Morning* has been interested in airing some of our footage. Of course, now that is out of the question, but we have excellent footage. The videographer in charge, Mike Burlington is his name, will be happy to work with your IT people since there are editing tools they may not be familiar with."

"That is terrific," said Lew, sitting straighter in her chair. "Can you give me some idea of what was taped and when?"

"Sure, Mike had three video cameras set up and running. One was a roving camera to record my staff as they strolled through the crowd giving away candy fishing lures or stopped to capture the kids getting ready to fish. Another was down on the dock to watch kids bring in the fish they'd caught and the awards ceremony.

"And he had a third camera set up on one of the awning supports to record the general public walking past the booth so we could show the scope of the event—how successful it has become. Chuck was so . . . proud of his tournament." The poor woman's voice cracked as she spoke. "There's no audio because we were planning to have an announcer do a voice-over, but the picture quality is excellent."

"All three videos may be helpful," said Lew, "especially that third one, the one that shows the people in the crowd going by the booth. How soon can we get this?"

"I'll have Mike send it over right away. But you need to let your IT people know that these are very large files. They aren't compressed like what you see on your phone. Watching them will take time. On the other hand, the good news is that you will be able to zoom in for close-ups if needed. Again, this is professional video and will require an experienced videographer like Mike to handle the editing tools."

"This is more than I had hoped for," said Lew. "I think that our IT person, her name is Dani Wright, should be able to access the files but I'm sure she'll need help from your videographer. Will he be available soon?"

"Right away. If you can transfer this call, I'll have him talk to Dani so they can get this going and . . . " Carlyn was quiet for a moment then said, "Jerry has made it very clear that whatever you people need to find out who—" She choked, unable to say more.

"It's okay," said Lew. "I understand. Please thank Jerry for taking care of this so quickly, will you? I'm transferring this call to Dani right now."

"Chief Ferris, that is going to be one mother lode of video," said Bruce after leaving Dani's office to return to Lew's. "And thank goodness because the videos that people sent in are not great. Well, no, I take that back. They are fine for the parents and grandparents but you aren't getting a good look at people milling around behind the subjects. And you cannot manipulate the visuals like we'll be able to now."

"Were you able to see anything in the ones sent in so far?" asked Osborne.

"The overwhelming majority of personal videos were of the parents and grandparents of the fifty children that had entered the contest. This was obvious from the focus on children posing with one or more adults."

Ray walked into the office while Bruce was talking. "How 'bout you, Ray, seen anything or anyone unusual?" asked Lew.

"Not yet, Chief," said Ray with a shake of his head. "I was just sitting down to watch with Bruce here when Dani got that video guy on the phone. But . . . I believe," he said with a tip of his head and an index finger raised high, "we will have puh-len-ty to see . . . shortly."

"Really?" Lew sounded like she was trying not to be too hopeful. "You seem pretty excited."

Ray dropped his banter. "Chief, I'll bet you the camera recording people passing by the Pfeiffer booth has better quality than a grade A surveillance video. If we can't see who approached Chuck Pfeiffer now . . . "

"Then why are you in here?"

"To let you know the video is streaming in and it's time we all sat down to watch like . . . right . . . now."

Five o'clock came and went. Six o'clock, too. At six thirty, Lew called a halt. "Okay, everyone, my eyes are glazing over. Let's pick up on this first thing in the morning."

Dani turned toward her with relief in her eyes. "Mike and I have a suggestion," she said, gesturing in the direction of the twenty-something man sitting beside her. "We have run through all the video from the cameras but Mike had it going at a faster-than-normal speed so you could decide what footage is the most important."

"I know what I would like to see and I would like to see it slowed down quite a bit," said Bruce. Ray and Osborne nodded in agreement. As they had been watching in silence, the flow of people had been constant and more than a little distracting as staff or Pfeiffer family members stood to walk in front of the cameras from time to time.

"So far we've seen no surprises," said Osborne. "The roving camera picked up the other booths and bystanders including the Lions Club, St. Mary's Auxiliary, and the elderly folks from the Senior Center. Then we got the Boy Scouts, the Girl Scouts, the Y, and all the teenage babysitters. None of that is critical to what we're looking for. Frankly, it's chaotic—hard to see anything other than too many bodies milling around."

"Hey," said Ray, "did you notice the Loon Lake Pub serving brewskis on property owned by the Tall Pines Tavern? Isn't that a violation of property rights?"

"Please don't mention that," said Lew. "I got enough on my plate. Speaking of which, isn't it time for dinner?"

"No," said Bruce, his moustache twitching—a tic familiar to Osborne as a sign that a pleasant thought had just entered the forensic scientist's psyche: "It's time to tighten our lines, doncha know."

The young videographer, Mike, looked confused by Bruce's remark.

"He means time to go fly-fishing," said Lew as she pushed back her chair and got to her feet.

"That may not be a bad idea. But on one condition, Mr. Peters. First, you deal with those two reporters who've been hanging out in the entrance hall. Tell them we're working with the videos sent in but haven't found anything significant yet; that we will be taking a break and they are welcome to return in the morning.

"While you do that, I will escape by the back door, rush home, and get my fishing truck and a peanut butter sandwich. Pick you up at the motel in half an hour?"

Bruce jumped to his feet. "You betcha, Chief."

"Doc, you interested?" asked Lew. "We'll hit the Coon River. I can use an hour or two in the water. Time to relax and think over what we've just seen."

Osborne smiled. Like Lew he often did his best thinking in the fishing boat or in the stream. "Count me in," he said. "I'll be at the motel with Bruce after I grab a bite, feed the dog, and get my fly rod."

"And while you people get your feet wet, I'm goin' to sit on my dock and watch dragonflies," said Ray. "Dani, Mike, you want to join me?" The two young people declined and guessing from the way their shoulders touched as they sat in front of Dani's computer screen, Osborne had a hunch they might end up having dinner together.

CHAPTER FOURTEEN

Wading up the Coon River from where Lew had parked her little white pickup and Bruce his SUV, Osborne was concerned that the water might be too warm for the fish to be feeding. He sure couldn't see a hatch of insects, which did not bode well for an evening of practicing his improved catch-and-release technique.

On the other hand, he knew that Lew had decided to fish the Coon River for two reasons: It was less than half an hour from town, and it held a sparkling run of riffles among the rocks and boulders where small but active native brook trout liked to hide. Even a magisterial brown trout deigned to show up from time to time.

More important, the stream was wide enough to satisfy Bruce, who was desperate for a lesson on his casting. "I'm so bummed," he'd said when he'd arrived the day before. "Not sure if I bought the wrong fly rod or my fly line and tippets are too heavy. But my casts are so sloppy, Chief, I'm embarrassed for anyone to see me. My dry flies land on the surface like they're made of rock—boom! Can't catch fish with that happening." He was so distressed. But Osborne was sympathetic: He'd been there and was forever grateful that the woman who often shared his breakfast table was an expert fly-fisher who didn't mind him tagging along in the stream.

"I am going to give you a midge fly, an adult, for you to try, Bruce," Lew was saying as she and Bruce waded a short distance behind Osborne. "With no other hatch tonight, this might work but use a 7X tippet if you have it." Osborne paused to watch as she handed him the pale olive dry fly, which she had tied.

"You sure?" asked Bruce. "I brought my stomach pump hoping I might catch something and see what insects it's got in its gut."

"Sweetie pie, forget the stomach pump," said Lew. "You've got plenty of trout food under those wading boots of yours. And why kill a trout to find that out anyway? Look at me, Bruce," she said, forcing him to stop and face her. "How would you like to have someone stick a stomach pump down your throat, through your esophagus, into your stomach, and suck out your dinner?"

The bushy eyebrows went up and Bruce gave a shrug with a sheepish look on his face. Sitting down on a nearby boulder, he bent to tie on a new tippet and the trout fly she had handed him. Getting to his feet, he raised his fly rod and cast forward with Lew watching.

"I'm doing something wrong, I know," he said, sounding frustrated. "I don't seem to be able to place my dry fly where I want it no matter how hard I try."

"And you are trying too hard, Bruce," said Lew. "How many times have I told you to stop muscling your way through the cast?"

"I dunno." Bruce dropped his fly rod to his hip and stood still with a pout on his face. "Maybe I'll give this up, get my spinning rod, and go fish with Ray."

"Okay, you'll do better with that fly rod of yours if you use an open-body stance, which is a lot more versatile for big guys like you," said Lew. "Watch me. Okay? Start by standing sideways to your target. Place your feet one ahead of the other with your left foot pointing at the target and your right foot dropped back at a 90-degree angle. Then with the power snap that I've taught you, I want you to shift your weight backward while keeping your elbow close to your body . . . like this . . . then finish the weight shift on the power snap as you follow through as usual. Right now you look like you're chopping wood when you should be moving like you're throwing a ball . . . "

Osborne was too familiar with the steps she was taking Bruce through. He had been there many times and still needed coaching, but bad as he was, Lew would say encouragingly, "It's okay, Doc, you'll still catch fish."

Wading upriver he left the student and teacher behind. As he moved through the water, the trees surrounding the creek reminded him how fortunate he was to live in a forested world of oak and aspen, maple and birch. Glimpsing a pine forest just around the next curve in the stream, he paused to admire the balsams whose elegant spires scratched the blue sky overhead.

"Doc," Lew's voice shattered his reverie. "Bruce and I are taking a break here on the big rock. Want to join us?"

In between bites of the roast beef sandwich he'd picked up at the KwikTrip on the drive out, Bruce said, "I've been thinking about the videos from the three cameras that we watched. I don't know about you two but I feel like there is something right smack in front of us and I'm not seeing it." He looked as dejected over the videos as he did his casting.

Lew patted him on the back. "I know, I know. We have to sit down tomorrow and go over those again minute by minute."

"I do have one idea," said Bruce, hesitating, "but it might cost some money . . . "

"This entire investigation is one hell of an expense already," said Lew. "Maybe that guy who called you from the governor's office might be willing to help out if we make a good proposal."

"This spring I attended a seminar run by the Wisconsin State Forensic Academy over in Milwaukee. They brought in this woman, Patience Merrill, who is an expert in visual perception and she walked us through the Milwaukee Art Museum where we would stop in front of a painting and have to tell her what we were seeing from something like the details of different objects or what facial expressions meant. We were given a set time to study the work of art and then write up a description of what we saw. The idea was to heighten our awareness of what we see when we approach a murder scene.

"The questions she had for us sounded simple at the beginning. For example, she would ask: 'What am I seeing here? What is the story behind this?' And, wow, the answers were all over the place. Really made you think hard and *look hard*."

"Bruce, are you serious? In an art museum you were learning how to view a crime scene?" asked Lew.

"You would be amazed at how different each of us in the group saw things in the paintings. What really struck me was how often there would be a detail so obvious—or so irrelevant (supposedly)—that none of us even mentioned it in our descriptions. What we missed was as important as what we saw."

As Osborne listened to the conversation, he remembered how in his late teens he loved studying art, especially studio art where he had had the opportunity to make several sculptures, got flattering feedback from the professor teaching sculpture, and had even flirted with the idea of pursuing sculpture as a career. That was until his father had looked at him in amazement and said, "Forget it, son, that is one hard way to make a living."

And so he had contented himself with dentistry, but he always felt a sense of pride when other dentists would compliment his work, especially his work in gold foil. And the truth was he had loved working with the models and materials of his profession. The precise line of a jaw, the elegance of a skull, still caught his eye.

"Bruce is on to something," said Osborne. "I think it's a fine idea. But is that woman somewhere that she can be reached?"

"And what will she charge us?" asked Lew. "Hundreds of dollars an hour?"

"I doubt that," said Bruce. "Her clients are medical students and business executives as well as federal and local law enforcement agencies. She can't charge too much or she won't get any business. These are not art collectors who are hiring her to teach them visual perception."

"And my next question is whether or not she might be available?" Lew was definitely interested.

With a sly twitch of his bushy moustache, Bruce reached into one of the right lower pockets in his fishing vest and pulled out his phone, which was carefully wrapped in plastic. Relishing the bated breath of the two people sitting beside him and watching, he slid the phone from its protective envelope, scrolled down his contact list, and pressed on a number that came up. He held a cautionary finger high while a phone rang somewhere.

"Hello, Patience," he said, "have I caught you in the middle of your dinner? No? Good. No, this isn't a personal call," he winked at Lew and Osborne. "I'm sitting on a rock in the middle of a trout stream with two law enforcement colleagues of mine . . . no, I am not making that up." He chuckled. "We have a question for you. Several in fact."

Five minutes later, he clicked the phone shut, slipped it back into the plastic envelope, and put the envelope into his pocket.

"Done," he said. "We caught her between assignments. She said she's off this week, visiting a sister in Madison, and she'll be here by eleven or so tomorrow morning. She also said to hold off on watching those videos until she gets here and works with us. She doesn't want us to be too familiar with the images."

"What did she say when you asked her what she would charge?"

"She estimated three full days of work and she'll charge us fifteen hundred plus mileage."

"Five hundred a day?" asked Osborne, worried that Lew was about to put the kibosh on hiring the woman. "That's a lot for the Loon Lake Police Department—"

"Hold your horses, Doc," said Bruce, sliding off the rock and standing up in the water. "I'll put a call in to the governor's office first thing in the morning and I'm sure we'll get the money. That's less than what I have to pay those two forensic techs who drove over from Green Bay."

With that Bruce stepped back with his right foot as he raised his fly rod preparing to backcast and let go with a perfect power snap and a smooth forward cast that dropped his midge onto a distant pool of quiet water without a sound. The tiny dry fly floated for less than a second before it was hit by an eager brook trout.

———◆———

Late that evening Osborne devoted half an hour to finishing the paint job on the windowsills in the downstairs room. Stepping back to assess the final effect, he was pleased. The room was lighter and felt spacious. All it needed now was the right equipment for tying flies. He knew better than to second-guess the supplies, even the tools, as Lew would want her own, but he felt confident that with some research he could find the right vise and maybe a few more items to complete his surprise. With that in mind, he set off to bed happy.

CHAPTER FIFTEEN

Beth slipped out of the house so early Tuesday morning that no one else in the family was awake yet. She had packed a banana and a yogurt in her tennis bag, which she planned to eat after spending an hour on the backboard working on her forehand before the kids arrived.

"Coach thinks I have a chance to be his number one singles player this fall if I can put more speed on the ball, Mom," she had told her mother the night before. "So my plan is to get to the courts by six thirty tomorrow morning. That'll give me plenty of time to practice, plus I'll have a basket of balls and can work on my serve, too."

"Sounds okay to me so long as none of the neighbors complain about the sound of tennis balls hitting the backboard before seven in the morning," her mother had said with a smile after Beth had explained why she would be out of the house so early the next morning. Having been grounded, she knew better than to leave the house without letting her parents know why.

The morning was overcast and the streets quiet as she strode along with her head down and shoulders set. Beth prided herself on having "a five-year plan" and that plan was to be the best tennis player on the girls' team, graduate in the top ten of her high school class, and go to Harvard, Stanford, or Williams College.

No one else in her class was planning to apply to those schools, but a boy from Milwaukee whose family had just moved to town had been telling her those were the best colleges in the country. And then he'd said he thought she was one of the few girls he'd met since he moved to Loon Lake who was smart enough to get accepted. That made Beth feel so good she was considering a crush on him even if he was four inches shorter.

She got to the tennis courts a few minutes after six, unpacked her racket and balls, and bounded onto the court with the backboard. Trees crowding the fence surrounding the courts worked as a windbreak and, she hoped against hope, deadened the sound so she wouldn't wake the neighbors. Apparently not as a half-hour flew by and no one showed up to complain.

She decided to get the basket of balls from the shed at the far end of the courts and practice serving until either the coach or some of the kids arrived. Walking to the shed she heard a car drive up and a door slam. Drats. She had hoped for another twenty minutes or so. Checking to see who was coming, she saw an older boy in jeans and a gray T-shirt coming her way. When he was close enough that she could make out the black stubble masking his lower face, she recognized him: the guy in the Jeep with Wendy, the one who had driven past her yesterday. Her stomach tightened.

"Hey, Beth," he said, "got a minute?"

"Not really—I'm teaching."

"You don't look like you're teaching." He glanced around as if to underscore there was no student in sight. "My name's Pete—Pete Bertrand. Wendy told me about you." Genial though his voice sounded, his eyes were so intent on hers that she had to resist feeling frightened.

"Oh?" She did her best to sound offhand.

"Got a proposal for ya." He held out a small dark green plastic baggie and Beth noticed he had scarlet and black tattoos running up both arms identical to the ones she'd seen on Wendy. "You know who in your crowd wants weed? You handle this for me and you get twenty-five percent. Could make you quite a few bucks. Wendy thinks you're probably well connected so should be easy-peasy. She likes you, too. How 'bout it?"

"No, thanks. I don't have time." She wanted to ease out of this without making the guy mad. "But tell Wendy thanks anyway."

"C'mon, just give it a try. You'll be surprised how easy it is—everybody wants some."

"Umm, why don't you let me think about it?" Beth felt like she was handling a snake.

"Okay. You think about it but don't tell anyone. You know better'n that, don't you?"

Another car door slammed and this time Beth saw her coach heading their way.

"I'll be by tomorrow," said the boy. "And, hey, anyone ever tell you you're cute?"

Oh God, thought Beth as he scurried off.

"Who the hell was that creep?" asked her coach when he reached the shed where Beth was still standing.

"I have no idea. I was practicing on the backboard and about to get the basket of balls when he showed up."

The coach studied her. "You look upset . . . "

"I'm okay . . . guess he scared me," she said, looking down and hitting her racket against the side of her sneaker.

"Well, don't come up here so early from now on, Beth. Too many trees around the courts—you can't be seen from the street. I don't want you up here alone. One of the girls on my team had someone come along that trail behind the trees and expose himself last summer. I sure don't want a repeat of that."

Walking home later that morning, Beth chose the long way to go. She didn't want to risk running into Wendy and her creep boyfriend again. As she neared her house, she thought she saw a Jeep Wrangler parked down the block. She ducked down the driveway then crept back to peer around the side of the porch but the car was gone. Maybe it was someone else's car?

Sheesh. She thought about telling her parents but what could they do? He hadn't touched her. And the fact that he talked to her about selling marijuana might get her in trouble all over again. You're a smart girl, Beth told herself; he shows up again you just say no, no, and no. He'll get the message.

CHAPTER SIXTEEN

At eleven A.M. Tuesday morning Patience Merrill arrived at the Loon Lake Police Department and was escorted by police chief Lewellyn Ferris to Dani Wright's office where two rows of chairs faced her computer screen, which was temporarily suspended from the ceiling to allow everyone a better view. Five people were waiting in the small room, including Osborne, Ray, Bruce, Dani, and Mike the videographer.

After introducing everyone, Lew said, "As I was telling you before she got here, we've asked Patience to help us with the videos Mike has been sharing. Her title may be 'visual perception expert,' but what that really means is she is skilled at helping us see beyond the obvious."

Speaking of which, "obvious" to Osborne was that Ray Pradt was close to swooning and he could see why. Patience could not have been much over thirty, which made sense as her résumé had her earning a PhD in the visual arts just three years ago. The young woman was a summery blonde with ice-blue eyes over wide cheekbones and peach-like cheeks. "Angelic" came to Osborne's mind as he studied her pleasant features.

Beneath a cropped, light brown jacket she wore a silk blouse the color of her eyes. Straight-legged tan slacks neatly belted at the waist implied a slender frame, and she carried herself with confidence.

"All right, everyone," said Patience. "Before we begin I want to make a big change here . . . you," she said, pointing to Ray, "you look like a good, strong guy. Can you help me raise this computer a few inches higher and tilt it forward so everyone can see okay?"

Ray got to his feet so fast he knocked two chairs over. Repressing a smile, Patience said, "Just a bit higher, Mr. Pradt; don't kill yourself." Ray blushed.

The shortest video, which was the one from the camera set low in the Pfeiffer booth in order to observe staff and family as they moved about or sat waiting was reviewed with no new observations except to show the brief time when Chuck Pfeiffer stood up, left the booth for about ten minutes, then returned to where he had been sitting. Osborne pointed out that would have been the time when Chuck had stopped to talk to him on his way back to the booth. Next was the video footage of the awards ceremony held down on the dock. "This will run maybe forty minutes," said Mike. "We were going for the ceremony itself—not the setup beforehand or any footage after the ceremony."

The video opened with Rikki Pfeiffer introducing the winners of the panfish contest followed by the winners of the walleye division. After she had given the walleye awards, there was a short lull during which the camera showed her stepping off to one side while waiting for the kids who had been fishing muskies to clamber up onto the stage.

"Wait," said Ray, leaning forward in his chair. "Can you back that up, Mike?"

As they watched, a figure appeared to the far left of the stage, barely visible until Rikki leaned over for a brief moment before standing again and walking to the center of the stage.

"Can you zoom in on that guy that she talks to?" asked Ray. "The one in the motorcycle jacket?" The image was enlarged on the screen and held.

"What do you see, Mr. Pradt?" asked Patience.

"Call me Ray, and I'm seeing someone who looks a lot like Jim Nickel—who *is* Jim Nickel, I'm sure. You agree, Doc?"

"Yep, that's Jim," said Osborne.

"Jim Nickel is Rikki Pfeiffer's ex-husband," said Ray. "Why would *he* be there?"

"Good question," said Lew. "An excuse to hang around his ex-wife?"

"Could he have a kid in the tournament?" asked Mike.

"Oh, no," said Ray, "his only kid is Bart Nickel. I'll bet you've met Bart, Mike. Before Chuck died, the rumor was he'd be replacing Jerry as CEO."

"Oh yeah, that guy," said Mike. "I've only seen him. But we did do a shoot with him and some staff for the company profile. I can find it if you need it."

"Not right now," said Patience. "I suggest we watch closely to see if his father appears again. You may recognize that individual more quickly now that you know what to look for. Everyone seems very interested in the fact that he is shown in this video. Am I right?" she glanced around the room and saw several heads nod.

"I imagine," she said, "that the first time everyone viewed this particular video all that you saw was Mrs. Pfeiffer and the children as they moved across the stage. Correct?" Again the nods. "You weren't focusing on images that may have reached your peripheral vision at that time."

They watched the rest of the video but the awards were predictable with no more sightings of the older man. Osborne was pleased to see that Mason handled receiving her shared third place award with aplomb. "She really caught a muskie?" asked Dani, impressed.

"A tiger muskie," said Osborne, "is the hybrid offspring of a muskellunge and northern pike. They tend to be smaller but good fighters and easier to catch. Mike, can I get a copy of this video, please? It will make a nice gift for her parents."

"You bet," said Mike and reached past Dani to start the third and final video.

"Hold on one second," said Lew. "Before we watch this one, I have a question. Ray or Doc, do either of you know how long Rikki and Jim have been divorced?"

"Since right after he went to prison," said Ray. "That would have been five years ago. I remember because Bart, their son, was still in college and I kicked him off the college fishing team, which I was coaching at the time. Suffice it to say I am not one of Rikki Pfeiffer's favorite people."

"How do you get kicked off a fishing team?" asked Patience.

"Cheating," said Ray. "You steal someone else's larger catch and substitute it for your own. Some folks I know will tell you cheating's a family tradition for that crew, which explains how the old man ended up in the hoosegow."

Osborne was quiet for a moment after Ray's remark before saying, "Interesting that Rikki and Jim may be in contact again. Most divorced couples I know avoid one another."

"O-o-h, I've known some that remarry," said Bruce. "My wife's parents did. Married twenty-two years, divorced for three, and remarried. Two years after that they divorced again." He chuckled.

"Think about it," said Lew. "Given what I've heard from the widow and the daughter-in-law, Chuck Pfeiffer's will has Rikki likely to inherit the bulk of the estate, which may include control of the company. So while it appears for the moment that Jerry Pfeiffer's position as CEO is safe, she will be in a position to make a significant change . . . "

"Like boot Jerry out and replace him with Bart?" asked Bruce. "Does that mean we have a 'person of interest' in Mr. Bart?"

"Nope. Bart has an ironclad alibi for where he was when Chuck was shot."

"As does Rikki," chimed in Ray. "She was up on stage with the rest of us during the time you think the killer pulled the trigger. Am I right?"

"Hold on, all of you. Would you please give me some background on what you are talking about?" said Patience. "I don't need details but enough to guide you as we watch the third video."

"The man who was murdered was in the process of rewriting his will and I've been led to understand that he may have been planning to significantly reduce how much he would be leaving his son, Jerry, and Jerry's family. Also he was about to promote his third and current wife's son, Bart, over Jerry, who has been CEO for the Pfeiffer company for the past five years. It's a large company with over seventy sporting goods stores across the Upper Midwest. Jerry was going to be forced into retirement with the CEO position going to his stepbrother. But Chuck died days before he could implement that change or finish rewriting his will."

"I see," said Patience, "so there was unrest in the ranks, to put it mildly?"

Everyone nodded.

"What I want to know," said Lew, "is the time noted on that video when we see Jim Nickel and compare that with where he was at the time that Chuck was murdered. Mike, can you help us determine the timing of the images we see on the video?"

"Easily," said Mike. "Our video software gives us a time stamp. I'll go back through that video and get you the exact time that he appears—and until he is no longer visible. Do you want me to do that right now or after we view the last video?"

"Later is fine," said Lew.

"Good," said Mike, "we'll get started. This video runs nearly two hours. I remember that we started shortly before one P.M. and didn't turn the camera off until three or so. I had the camera rigged to one of the struts holding the canopy over the booth so we could catch the crowds going by the Pfeiffer booth during the busiest hours of the tournament. Carlyn and I wanted to show the variety of people, how involved and happy they were that day—everything that would make Chuck proud that he had launched this tournament that people loved."

"One more thing before we watch this," said Lew. "Ray, will you see what you can find out about Jim Nickel? See if any of your miscreant friends have run into him recently—at the bars? Heard him say what he's been up to?" She pursed her lips in thought. "I mean, why is that guy hanging around a kids' fishing tournament? Given what a beautiful day it was and Nickel was there with his motorcycle buddies—shouldn't they have been out riding?"

"Will do," said Ray. "But I might have to buy some weed to get in the good graces of my bad buds, doncha know. Any chance the Loon Lake PD can cover my costs?" He winked. Lew gave him the dim eye. She knew he was only half kidding. Maintaining his "bad boy" status gave Ray access to a social circle sensitive to people asking too many questions. And that circle of Ray's was often right where the answers were.

———◆———

The two hours seemed to speed by. When the video ended, the room was silent.

"I didn't see any sign of Jim Nickel," said Ray, sounding disappointed.

"I didn't see anyone with a gun who might have shot Chuck," said Lew. "And I was watching so close . . . It must have happened, the camera must have caught it, but I sure as hell didn't see a thing. I mean, we see Chuck sitting there, don't we?"

"He didn't move a lot," said Bruce. "I saw him shake hands and chat with people but he didn't stand up or walk around except for that one ten-minute period when Doc said he had stopped over to chat with him. Otherwise the guy stayed put.

"All I saw was the right side of his face as he would turn to talk to people going by," said Osborne. "Wasn't he shot behind the right ear?"

"Let's watch it again. There must be something," said Bruce.

"Okay, people," said Patience walking to the front of the room to face them, the computer monitor above her to her right, "you have—every one of you—committed the cardinal sin: *you watched for what you wanted to see.*"

"Geez Louise, of course we did," said Lew.

"Let me give you an example. What you did is similar to a management consultant going into a planning meeting between two different groups—say, emergency management and the health department—with each group having their own priorities, but *your goal is to help them learn to work together.*

"If you go in with *your* questions and you get *your* questions answered, are you happy? Of course *you* are. You haven't isolated the true quandary: The fact that *emergency management is not communicating with the health department and vice versa.* So, yes, you got both groups answering your questions. But no one noticed whether they were listening to each other. And if they don't listen to one another, they cannot work together."

"How does that apply to this?" asked Lew. "I'm confused."

"We will watch this video again," said Patience. "I want each of you to stop looking for a person with a gun or a man in a motorcycle jacket. This time, you jot down as fast as you can on the notepad that I am handing you only what you actually see—not what you expect to see, not what you hope to see. Just the reality: kids on tricycles, moms with diaper bags, someone blowing their nose—just detail, detail, detail. Make no assumptions.

"If someone stops to chat with Chuck Pfeiffer, what do they look like? Do they laugh? Do they walk by more than once? Don't watch Chuck, watch the crowd."

"What about staff or family in the booth?"

"Everyone. We'll watch this now and then I want your notes. We'll meet again in the morning and we'll talk. We may watch it all again or I may highlight certain sections or frames for us to review."

Lew's cell rang. She listened and clicked off. "Sorry, have to go. That was Officer Todd Martin. There's been a burglary at the Northern Lights Nursing Home. We'll have to look at the video later or first thing in the morning. Doc, Bruce, do you mind coming with me? Todd said there's been money, drugs, and guns stolen. He's got thirty-four residents who say their rooms were broken into. I'll need as much help as I can get."

"Guns? From a nursing home?" Bruce was astonished.

As they hurried from the building, Osborne heard Ray invite Patience to dinner. He couldn't hear her response.

CHAPTER SEVENTEEN

When Osborne and Lew arrived at the nursing home, they found the residents gathered in the dining hall—all thirty-four, including seven in wheelchairs. Moving among them and taking notes was Officer Martin followed by the administrator, Elizabeth Herre.

"Oh, Chief Ferris, I can't believe this has happened," said Elizabeth Herre. She looked like she was about to break into tears. "We have security locks on all our entrances—"

"So someone broke in from outside—is that what happened?" asked Lew just as Todd Martin walked up. "Where exactly? We may be able to get fingerprints . . . "

"No, Chief, I'm afraid Mrs. Herre is wrong," said Todd. "It was an inside job." Bruce moved closer to hear what the young officer had to report. "Almost every apartment in the complex is missing something—loose cash, guns, medications. Whoever did it knew where to look, too."

"Really?" asked Lew. "How was that managed? How do you get thirty-four elderly people out of their rooms at the same time, for heaven's sake?"

"A group of high school kids gave a concert here this afternoon. It lasted two hours and everyone attended. Right, Mrs. Herre?"

The woman nodded. "We hold these events once a month and they are very popular. But I'm sure Officer Martin is wrong. I can't imagine anyone on our staff—"

"Are we talking painkillers like morphine, OxyContin? Any of those stolen?" asked Bruce, butting in.

"Oh yes," said Todd. "Along with some Percocet and Percodan. Not good. Stolen from the small pharmacy they have here. Someone had a key to the cabinet holding those drugs."

"Only two people on my staff plus myself have keys," said Elizabeth. "I just can't imagine who could have done this."

Lew glanced over at Todd. "And what's this about guns? How many guns are we talking about?"

"Fifteen handguns, Chief. They're missing Rugers, .357 Magnums, Sig Sauers, Glocks, you name it. Turns out a number of the people living here—and this is men *and women*—have been taking firearm training courses with follow-up target practice once a week at the Loon Lake Shooting Gallery."

"Are you kidding me? Why on earth?" asked Lew.

A reedy female voice piped up: "Don't you watch the news? You've got radicals, you've got crazies, you've got all these drug addicts breaking into people's homes to steal their medicines. It's an epidemic for goodness' sakes. Didn't you hear about the hospice center over in Minocqua that just got robbed of their drugs? Just because we're old doesn't mean we don't want to be safe.

"We knew this was going to happen," she muttered.

"Lot of good your guns did you," said Bruce, making sure to walk away before the woman could respond.

Osborne recognized the figure behind the voice: Harriet McClellan. A close friend if not a mentor of his late wife's, he had forgotten she moved into a nursing home shortly before he retired. *Geez Louise,* he thought, *Harriet must be nearly ninety years old.* And while she had once been a statuesque five feet eight inches tall, now she was the size of a sparrow.

"Why, Harriet McClellan," said Osborne. "I had no idea you were living out here."

"Fifteen years, Paul, fifteen years. But I'm holding on," she cackled as she tucked her shrunken body into an armchair that could have held three of her.

He wasn't surprised. She had never struck him as soft or weak. Quite the contrary: She was dry as a sheet of parchment and just as strong. After the untimely deaths of her husband and son as well as the loss of McClellan's Sport Shop, she had managed to maintain a formidable presence in Loon Lake, serving for years as president of the Loon Lake Garden Club and rarely missing the weekly meetings of the by-invitation-only bridge club of which Osborne's late wife had been proud to be a member.

Aware that Lew, Bruce, and Todd were still busy questioning the residents as to what each had had stolen from their rooms or apartments, he hurried to catch up and do his share. Pulling out a notepad from his back pocket, he raised his pen and asked, "So, Harriet, can you tell me what was stolen from your apartment, please?"

"Why would I tell you? You're a dentist, Paul. I want to talk with that woman what's-her-name."

"You mean police chief Lewellyn Ferris? Well, you certainly may but I'm also helping out at the moment and Chief Ferris appears to have her hands full." He pointed toward Lew who was across the room and bent over talking to an elderly man who was also in a wheelchair. Unconvinced, Harriet gave him a hostile stare.

Patiently (in the tone he had always used to explain to patients why the tooth needed to be extracted in order to avoid a severe infection) he explained how he had been deputized to help with the forensic odontology on previous cases and added, "So given Loon Lake has a small three-person police force—and I'm retired from my dental practice—I volunteer to be deputized and help out when they're short-handed. As they are right now, Harriet. So do you mind answering my question?"

"Well, alright," she said, holding her head to one side as if she smelled something bad. Osborne resisted a grin. Harriet might be old but she was haughty as ever. Her attitude reminded him of a comment one of his McDonald's coffee crowd had made about her years ago: "You have to hand it to Harriet McClellan. That woman's got an even disposition all right: Even when she laughs it's at the expense of someone else."

"I had my bingo winnings in my top dresser drawer and that's gone," Harriet was saying in a grudging tone. "Twenty dollars— two bills. And my gun, which is a valuable antique. I've owned it for years. A gift from Bob before he died. Remember when those motorcycle hoods came through town? He wanted me to feel safe.

"You remember my husband, Bob, and Martin, too, don't you, Paul?"

"Of course I do, Harriet, although Martin was a few years ahead of me."

"Well, Martin remembered you. I know. He often mentioned how you and your father were such good customers of our shop." Her eyes got a distant look as she said, "Your father was such a lovely man. If only . . . " Osborne did not want to hear where that thought was going.

"Yes, I miss Dad, too, but, um, Harriet, can you describe the gun that was stolen?" He was determined to get her back on track as soon as possible.

"Oh, it's a lovely little handgun. One of those teeny ones you can carry in your purse. I would be so happy to have it back."

"Anything else taken besides the money and your gun?"

"No. All I keep in my drawer beside the gun is my blood pressure medicine and whoever it is didn't want that."

While she was talking, Osborne was experiencing a rush of sensations, none of them pleasant. The sound of her voice with its hint of superciliousness brought back memories of the mean-spirited comments Mary Lee would repeat after her bridge club gatherings: vicious gossip about other women in Loon Lake—many of them his patients—and always remarks that had originated with Harriet. More than once the gossip turned out to be false but that was after one of Harriet's targets had been ostracized from future bridge games or garden club events.

Equally disturbing was that even as he was surprised to run into Harriet at the nursing home, he was beginning to feel that he had recently seen her somewhere . . . but where?

"Excuse me, Doc," said Lew, who had appeared at his elbow. "Elizabeth has pulled the staff into her office and we need to take a few minutes with them. They may know something."

There were four nurses on duty at this time and they didn't know much. "We were all watching the concert, too," said a dark-haired woman. Her nametag indicated her name was Marcie. "Well, wait, I did see Wendy come out of a room down the hall. Not sure why she was there. I thought she was getting off early today."

"I wouldn't worry about Wendy," said Elizabeth. She looked at Lew, "She's a CNA on staff here. I would expect her to be checking on the rooms, it's her job."

"And a CNA is what?" asked Bruce.

"Certified nursing assistant." Elizabeth lowered her voice, "I'm afraid we assign our CNAs a lot of the cleaning when needed. Not the most fun job in the building."

"Why isn't she in this meeting right now?" asked Lew. "I asked you to have all the staff here."

"She's off right now," said Elizabeth. "Her shift ended at three. Do you want me to call her and have her come back? Otherwise, she'll be in at six tomorrow morning."

"I guess that won't be necessary," said Lew, "but please have her call me when she gets in tomorrow morning. I want to be sure we've spoken with everyone who might have seen something today."

"Certainly," said Elizabeth. "What time do you want her to call? If she's here at six won't that be a little early?"

"No, that's fine. I'll be in my office by then. Oh, one more question. Do any of your CNAs have keys to the drug cabinet?"

"Absolutely not," said Elizabeth. She looked around the room at the four women standing there. "No one besides myself, Marcie, and Jocelyn have keys to the drug cabinet. Right?"

"Yes," said the four simultaneously.

"We keep that cabinet locked at all times," said Marcie.

"We're all registered nurses," said Elizabeth, "and that level of security is required in order to have in-house access to the drugs."

"I see. All right, everyone, thank you for your help. I want to give you this," she said as she handed each a small piece of paper. "This has my cell phone number on it in case you think of something that may be of help. Please don't hesitate to give me a call."

———◆———

Driving back with Lew in the cruiser, Osborne puzzled over where he might have run into Harriet McClellan. They were pulling into the parking lot at the police department when it dawned on him: "Lewellyn, that elderly woman I was talking to, she's in the video from the tournament—" His voice rose.

"Doc," said Lew, glancing over at him as she turned off the ignition, "settle down. That whole goddamn nursing home crowd is in the video. They were all sitting in the booth run by the Senior Center. Didn't you notice?"

"Oh." He relaxed back against the seat. "Guess I was watching all the wrong people."

Lew reached over and patted his hand. She gave him an indulgent smile. "You'll see tomorrow morning when we run through that video again. I think we'll all be surprised at what we see this next time."

"Sure you're right. Don't suppose you would be interested in a pizza at my place later? It is Tuesday, you know." They had fallen into a pattern of Tuesdays at his place, Thursdays and some Sundays at hers.

She gave him a grin as she sat thinking. "Well, okay. I'll be exhausted so if you don't mind an early bed evening—"

"Count on it," he said, tired but pleased himself.

They slept that night with all the windows open as the temperature dipped into the low sixties and made snuggling a must. Light breezes carried the soothing hoots of owls as the moon slipped silver beams through the spiky needles of the red pines guarding the shore.

A cell phone rang in the dark. Osborne struggled up from a deep sleep not sure what he had heard but Lew was already on her phone. He heard her ask in a sleep-laden voice, "Marcie? What is it? No, yes, it's late but that's fine. Why are you calling?"

Lew touched the speaker button so Osborne could hear.

"I am so sorry, Chief Ferris. I thought I would get your voicemail. Why don't I call back in the morning?"

"Marcie, please, tell me why you're calling."

"I remembered something after our meeting and I couldn't sleep. It was a couple weeks ago and our CNA, Wendy Stevenson, asked if she could borrow my keys to get into the storage room at the back of the building. She had them for over an hour before I remembered to ask for them back. Chief Ferris, the key to the drug cabinet was on the ring with my other keys. And one of the keys is a master for the building. This has been bothering me all night . . ."

"I see," said Lew. "You didn't happen to notice if she left the building with your keys?"

"No, I mean, I didn't notice. I was caring for one of our residents who was recovering from a stroke that day so I didn't pay attention. And, um, thing is that girl is weird. She has problems."

"Problems?"

"I think she drinks or maybe she does drugs. I don't know but she's weird."

"Hmm, I am scheduled to talk with her first thing in the morning," said Lew. "Given what you're saying, I'll stop out at the nursing home and meet with her in person."

"I'm probably wrong and being unfair," said Marcie.

"But it could be important information so thank you for calling, Marcie. Now get some sleep."

"You, too, Chief Ferris. And sorry to call so late."

Lew clicked off her phone and lay back in the bed, her body tense. "Do you need to get up?" asked Osborne. "Want some coffee?"

"At three thirty in the morning? Not sure what good that'll do. No, Doc, I'll try to get some sleep."

"We'll both try." He slipped an arm across her shoulders and hoped the soft lapping of the lake against the shore would help her sleep.

CHAPTER EIGHTEEN

Beth hesitated before she sliced a banana into her cereal. Should she maybe go back to bed instead of the early morning practice she had been planning? It still bothered her that that creepy Pete had shown up at the tennis court yesterday morning. But Summer Sectionals were three days away and she was desperate to work on her serve.

Shrugging, she went ahead and sliced the banana. The more she thought about it, the more she was convinced that she'd been so unfriendly to the guy he wouldn't dare bug her again. No, she'd be fine. Plus she had been getting to the courts a little later than usual. If he did go by at the same time as yesterday, she wouldn't be there.

Happy with that thought, Beth wiped her hands, grabbed her tennis bag, and slipped out the front door without making a sound. As she walked down the street toward the path she liked to take across the courthouse green, Rich Gibbson, their next-door neighbor, was backing out of his driveway.

"Hey, young lady, where are you off to?"

"Hi, Mr. Gibbson, the tennis courts up at the high school."

"Well, jump on in and let me give you a ride."

"Thanks," she gave him a big smile as she hopped in. Three minutes and a friendly chat later she was skipping toward the storage shed to get the hopper of tennis balls.

A chipmunk skittered across the court behind her as Beth walked along gathering tennis balls into the hopper. It had been a good hour and she was happy with where her serve was going. Faster and harder, for sure. So long as she remembered to keep her left arm up, step back, and drop that racket head—

She froze. Did something move behind those birch trees? Bordering the court on her right was a stand of five mature birches, leaves swaying like a bright green scarf against the white trunks, which were slashed with horizontal black stripes.

Alert and worried, Beth turned to her left as if she was about to serve then quickly dropped her racket to turn around. Yes, there was a figure in black standing very still among the birch trees: Pete Bertrand.

Unnerved, she checked her watch. Twenty minutes until coach arrived. Maybe, she hoped, a parent will drop a kid off early. She decided to pretend she hadn't seen anything and continue to pick up the tennis balls. If he moved toward her, she would run across the field to the high school entrance where she might be able to find a janitor.

Ducking her head as she punched balls into the hopper, Beth didn't look up again. She didn't want to see the man hiding in the trees. She didn't want him to know she had seen him.

It wasn't until she had hurried up to the shed to drop off the hopper that she dared to look back. No movement by the birches. He was gone.

Oh my god, she thought. *I should tell my parents . . . but I can't. If I tell them who he is, they'll want to know how he knows me and I'll have to confess that I lied to that girl and that's why he thinks I could sell stuff for him. And that would be so embarrassing. They'd think I'm really dumb.*

Things were bad enough at home already: Everyone doted on Cody just 'cause he's a boy and they think he's so cute. Well, he's not that cute—he's a pain in the butt. Then there's Mason—such a little jerk always fussing with fishing poles and pretending she's some great sportswoman like their mom. Next thing you know she'll brag she can shoot and dress a deer.

No one cares about her tennis or her dance classes. And now she's supposed to tell them she lied? Beth wanted to cry.

———◆———

A block down the road, Pete Bertrand climbed into his Jeep pleased with what he had just seen. What a beautiful girl! And she was interested. Why else would she have shown up this morning? He didn't want to come on too strong until he had a plan. But this was cool: She had seen him and she did not get angry or fake anger like she did yesterday. That was just a cover 'cause that coach guy was walking up.

All he had to do now was to dump Wendy. God, he was tired of her. But she just pulled off a great job for him—all those guns and the drugs. He better think this through. But so far, whoa, life is going well. He reached back into the wooden box behind his seat for one of his favorite little white pills and cranked up the radio. Hoo-haa, man, is this day off to a great start.

———◆———

"Gosh, Doc, I didn't know what to say," said Ray. "Patience told me she hates people who fish." He was cradling his coffee cup, which Osborne had just refilled for the third time and it was only six thirty in the morning. Lew had been up and gone for over an hour. The knock on the back door from his neighbor had come shortly after six. And Ray was beside himself.

"She told me she read this book *What a Fish Knows* and discovered fish have all these feelings and memories and—bottom line—I'm committing murder when I catch fish. Oh, and she refuses to eat 'em, too."

"Sounds to me like she hasn't given your sautéed walleye a chance," said Osborne. He chuckled.

"It's not funny, Doc. She means it."

"In that case, you aren't meant for each other. Sounds pretty straightforward to me."

The expression on Ray's face was morose. "But, Doc, she's one of the most interesting women I've met in years. And as pretty as a forget-me-not. Doc, I don't want to let this one go."

"Spoken like a true fisherman. Ray." Osborne leaned forward to emphasize his next words, "She is not the woman for you. You fish, you love to fish, you love to eat fish. You are an expert muskie fisherman—give it up."

"Maybe I can find us a compromise . . . "

"Sure, catch and eat small children instead."

"This isn't funny, Doc."

"I'm sorry but wise as she might be helping us with the videos, I'm not sure Patience lives in the real world. Or *our* real world anyway. What did she order for dinner last night?"

"Squash ravioli."

"Hmm. Have you told her flowers talk? She should consider the feelings of squash blossoms."

"Now you're screwing with my head, Doc."

"Yes, I am. Look, Ray, I respect the woman and her point of view. After all, Lew has taught me the importance of catch-and-release. But she sounds like she carries her concern for fish to an extreme."

"Wait," Ray raised his right index finger, which Osborne had learned long ago signaled an important thought. "Doc . . . that is . . . the answer."

"Not sure I know what you mean."

"I . . . will instruct Ms. Patience Merrill . . . in . . . the art of . . . catch-and-release." Ray's face lit up. "That'll do it. I'm sure. But, um, remind me of the basics."

"Sure: Keep the fish wet. You want to land a fish in the water and hold it in the water or close to the water with wet hands. If you have to net a fish, use a rubber net as they have the least impact on a fish. Once you catch a fish, always use forceps to remove the barbless hook to minimize handling the fish."

"I like this: 'Catch-and-release' here I come." Ray looked so hopeful, Osborne hated to ruin his morning.

"Okay, but that doesn't sound to me like a 'catch in a skillet.' And you are all about eating fish whether it's walleye, bluegill, or muskie. Plus, you can't possibly land a muskie using a barbless hook. Ray, no matter how smart and lovely the lady is, I don't think you can change who you are."

Ray's eyes clouded. "I'll keep working on this . . ."

"That said, we're due to review that video starting at nine this morning," said Osborne, glancing up at the kitchen clock. "See you there."

———————

When Osborne walked into Dani's office at nine that morning, everyone was waiting. Everyone except police chief Lewellyn Ferris.

CHAPTER NINETEEN

It was seven fifteen Wednesday morning and Lew was intent on getting through the paperwork that seemed to be multiplying like loaves and fishes since Chuck Pfeiffer's death. The fact that the bulk of the documents were computerized didn't make life any easier. Just as she decided to take a short break and refill her coffee cup, Dispatch rang her desk phone.

"Chief, just got a 911 call from the Northern Lights Nursing Home and EMTs are on their way—suspected drug overdose. Thought you should know." Lew hung up and checked her cell for Elizabeth Herre's number.

"Chief Ferris, I'm on my way to the emergency room," said the woman in a brisk voice.

"Can you tell me more?" asked Lew.

"All I know is one of our CNAs, Wendy Stevenson, was found unconscious in her car in the parking lot about ten minutes ago. She had arrived at work at six, right on time, but about a half-hour later she said she needed a break. One of my nurses on staff this morning said she didn't look good when she arrived and seemed disoriented. Sorry, I'm pulling into the hospital parking lot."

"I'll meet you there," said Lew.

Pulling into the parking area for the emergency room, Lew saw the EMTs unloading a gurney. Standing nearby and watching was Elizabeth Herre. "Do we know more?" asked Lew, walking up and following her into the emergency waiting room.

"Yes, they found two pill containers in her car. Not only did she take oxycodone but the containers are two of the ones stolen from our pharmacy."

"Do we know how she got those?"

"No idea yet. But I have her purse, which she left in our building. One of my nurses grabbed it so we can see if there's any information on her family. Who to call and let them know she's in bad shape."

"You don't have that on file?"

"We thought we did but the name and phone number for the close relative that she put on her application form doesn't work. Got a message that the phone number is invalid. I hope she's going to be okay . . . "

Lew walked up to the receptionist at the emergency room desk and showed her badge.

"Yes, Chief Ferris," said the young woman manning the desk. "I'll let Dr. Reich know you're here. He's the doc on duty and he's with the patient right now. I'm sure he'll be out to speak with you soon."

Lew sat down next to Elizabeth who was rifling through a tan vinyl bag covered with studs and fringe. She brought up a worn red wallet, a pair of loose sunglasses, a lipstick case, two tubes of mascara, a set of car keys for a Toyota, and another ring with seven keys on it. Elizabeth studied the ring of keys then reached into her own purse and pulled out an identical ring. She held them side by side on her lap so Lew could see.

"They match," said Elizabeth quietly. "This one is a master key that works in the doors to all our apartments, this opens the front entrance deadbolt, and these four work for the kitchen, our supply room, our nurses' private bathroom, and the computer room. But this one," she held up one key that was smaller than the others, "this is the key to the drug cabinet in the pharmacy."

"Marcie called me during the night to say she remembered Wendy borrowing her keys several weeks ago. Are you sure these are identical to yours? I'm going to have them double-checked."

Elizabeth handed her the ring of keys. "I'll be very surprised if they aren't. She must have run out and had Marcie's keys copied."

"Or someone was waiting near your building and ran off to copy them for her."

The emergency room physician emerged from the ICU unit and beckoned them to join him in a small room off the waiting area. "She's very confused and hallucinating but her vitals are stable," he said. "We'll be able to release her in about four hours or so."

"I'll have Officer Roger Adamczyk here to keep her under surveillance until then," said Lew. "Once she is released, we'll be putting her under arrest."

The physician nodded, then said, "She's lucky her reaction was as treatable as it is. The EMTs were able to give her Narcan, which is an overdose antidote."

It was nine thirty when Lew finally made it to Dani's office. The room was darkened and quiet with everyone watching the video projected overhead. Seeing Lew walk in, Patience hit the pause button and said, "Good morning, Chief Ferris, we're reviewing the two-hour video that shows people moving past the Pfeiffer booth. If it is okay with you, we'll keep moving forward. I'll pause it every few minutes for us to discuss what we are seeing. I'll be starting it over, too."

"Any news, Chief?" asked Bruce before Patience started the video.

"We'll be arresting one of the nursing home staff for the thefts yesterday. She arrived at work high and with what appears to be keys to all the rooms in the place including the drug cabinet in the pharmacy. And she had some of the stolen drugs on her."

"That was easy," said Bruce.

"Let's hope it's as easy as it sounds. I've sent Todd Martin out to search her apartment for the missing drugs and guns and everything else she took. Assuming we find everything—then I can relax."

"Are you ready for me to play the video?" asked Patience.

"Before you do," said Lew, glancing around the room, "is there anything new that you've all seen so far? Any sign of Jim Nickel?"

"No sign of Mr. Nickel but I got an update on the guy you might find interesting," said Ray, tipping back in his chair. "Hanging out late last night at the Pied Piper Tavern and who walked in but Buddy Drummell, my best bass guy. Haven't seen that joker in months and now I know why: He's been in the slammer."

"What does that mean—'bass guy'?" asked Patience.

"Oh, that's right, you don't fish," said Ray. "I have clients who want to fish bass and Buddy knows right where to find smallies. And they are the best fighters, those smallies. I got a client from Detroit all he wants to fish are smallies and—"

"Fine," said Lew, interrupting. "What's the deal with Buddy Drummell? Why has he been incarcerated?"

"Well, Buddy's not the sharpest knife in the drawer and he sort of forgot to tell the IRS that his folks had passed away—forgot for three years and kept cashing their Social Security checks."

"That'll do it," said Lew. "And?"

"So he's just out of the halfway house over on Dahl Street where Jim Nickel has been living these last three months." The room was quiet. "Turns out Jim's got a regular visitor—Miss Rikki."

"Mrs. Pfeiffer, you mean," said Lew.

"Yes. She's been dropping by every couple weeks with his favorite lemon meringue pie."

"Really? She doesn't strike me as a woman who cooks," said Lew.

"I have no idea if she made 'em or not," said Ray, "but Buddy said she would drop in with pie for the guy. And turns out that when they were all chewing the fat, Jim let it be known that once he was out that he'd be back in the game big time."

"Back working, you mean?" asked Lew.

"Yep. Told the boys in the house that his kid had a big job with the Pfeiffer Corporation and he'd be finding a place for the old man."

"That's interesting," said Lew. "Very interesting."

"There's more. He said that old man Pfeiffer had an aortic aneurysm that could blow any time. And when it did who knows what could happen—"

"Meaning he could be helping his son run the show?" asked Lew.

"Buddy got that impression, but like I said: Buddy isn't the brightest."

Osborne decided to ask the question: "What if Jim Nickel got tired of waiting for the aneurysm to blow?"

"Doc has a point," said Lew. "What we haven't considered— what *I* haven't considered is this: We know Jim Nickel is not the most upstanding citizen. Correct?" Everyone nodded. "We know he is recently out of prison, and white collar or not, it is still prison. Given that he may be in the position to make money soon—"

"Wait," said Ray, "in a position to have an ex-wife with a LOT of money baking him pies . . . "

"Why not hire someone to do his dirty work?" Lew's question hung in the air. "All right, folks, time to watch closely."

As Lew spoke, Patience gave Mike a nod to start the video running. Two minutes into the video, Ray said, "Do you believe how much ice cream there is in our world? It's a wonder some of these people don't weigh four hundred pounds."

"Between ice cream and bratwurst, you'd think we were watching Food Network Northwoods," said Osborne. "I'm beginning to regret giving up my practice. After what I've seen this morning, Loon Lake's dentists will be besieged with cavities."

"Yeah, in people of all ages," said Ray. "Whoever said they came to watch kids fish? Hell, they came to pig-out. Wait, I think—Mike, can you back the video up a minute or two?"

"Sure."

Lew wondered what he had seen because she hadn't caught anything unusual. Thanks to bright sunshine on the morning of the tournament, the images on the screen were well lit and colorful making it hard to miss much. And Ray had made a good point: Everyone walking by the booth—parents, little kids, older kids, middle-age couples, people walking, kids on bikes and trikes—*everyone* was either licking an ice cream cone, cramming popcorn into their mouths, or finishing off something in a hot dog bun.

Aside from people inhaling food, the camera caught Chuck Pfeiffer's head and shoulders from the back. Lew could see that he had rested his right arm on a small table just inside a knee-high curtain framing the booth. Even though his face couldn't be seen, his body language was that of a man relaxed and happy to watch the people passing by. When the occasional passerby waved or said something to him, he responded with nods and waves and appeared to be enjoying himself.

She could also see action in the booth off to the far right, which was run by the Lions Club and where hot dogs, bratwurst, and popcorn could be seen being delivered from one set of hands to another. Directly across the way was a large booth run by the Senior Center.

As they waited for Mike to back up the video, Lew realized that during her first viewing she hadn't paid attention to the people in the booths. Now, determined to look beyond the faces of people passing by, she recognized several residents of the Northern Lights Nursing Home.

"Wow," she said to no one in particular after Mike had backed the video up, "I had no idea there were that many people over in the Senior Center booth."

"What you really mean is how many people you missed seeing before," said Patience, sounding pleased to prove her point.

"It's quite something once you really look," said Osborne. "I see half a dozen people I know."

As he spoke, Mike zoomed in on the distant booth where people in the booth were up and moving to position chairs and wheelchairs while handing binoculars back and forth. "They're getting ready for the awards ceremony," said Mike. "We're about five minutes from the end of this video because I turned the camera off while we were taping Rikki handing out the awards."

"Wow, those folks came equipped," said Bruce.

"You better believe it," said Osborne. "This tournament is a highlight of the summer for some of the old folks. Between cameras and binoculars they weren't going to miss a moment—especially if they were watching their grandchildren—"

"Or great-grandchildren," said Dani with a laugh.

As they watched, Lew saw a surge in the number of people passing by. "Why do I see so many more people walking past Chuck Pfeiffer all of a sudden?" she asked no one in particular.

"They're moving down to the dock area to watch the awards being handed out. I asked Mr. Pfeiffer if he didn't want to move, too, but he said he'd just sit where he was and watch the video later."

"There! See that?" Ray jumped to his feet as a trio of men in black leather jackets moved along in the crowd. "That's Jim Nickel right there." Ray pointed.

"Yes, but he's nowhere near Chuck Pfeiffer," said Bruce. "The autopsy report came in this morning and there's no question but that the bullet came from a gun held tight to the head. The guy you're pointing out is walking by from a distance."

Ray leaned forward, focused on the parade of people. "Just watch. He'll make his move."

While everyone kept a close eye on the three men in black, Osborne saw what looked like a forest gnome sidling through the crowd. The petite figure wore a long-sleeved dark jacket that hung to its knees, and a canvas bag, along with a pair of binoculars, was slung across its chest. A wide-brimmed khaki hat obscured the facial features. Male or female? Osborne couldn't tell.

The gnome stood out against the summery colors worn by the other tournamentgoers as it moved sideways through the flow of the crowd toward the Pfeiffer booth where it paused beside Chuck, leaned over his head, and reaching out its left arm gave him a hearty slap on the shoulder followed by a playful ruffle of his hair.

Chuck threw his head back—in surprise or to avoid another too-friendly gesture—as his visitor leaned again to whisper into his right ear before moving off with a wave of one hand. Before the figure disappeared into the crowd, it stopped and turned to look at Chuck once more but all that Osborne could make out of a face beneath the floppy brim of the hat was a chin. A pale, firm chin.

"Did you see that?" he asked.

"Did I see *what?*" asked Ray, irritated that his suspect in the black leather jacket had passed by without pulling a gun and shooting anyone. The last view of Jim Nickel had him swigging from a can of beer.

It took two more viewings of the video for everyone to see the figure Osborne had seen. The entire interaction between that person and Chuck Pfeiffer took less than sixty seconds—and it was preceded and followed by so many other people nodding toward him or extending a hand to shake his that the episode didn't stand out. Zooming in didn't help, either.

"Seems pretty inconsequential to me," said Lew.

"But a good eye, Dr. Osborne," said Patience from where she was sitting behind Osborne. "You have a very good eye." Osborne knew when he was being humored.

They all sat through another viewing of the awards ceremony after which Mike offered to play the video of the crowd scene moving past the Pfeiffer booth again.

"Heavens, no. This is enough for today," said Lew, rubbing her eyes. "I wish we had seen more and I'm sure we've missed something—"

"Before you give up on it," said Patience, "I suggest Mike give Chief Ferris the time stamps for the Nickel gentleman entering and leaving and the time stamps for the figure in the sun hat. Both of those sequences occur, I believe, close to the time during which it is believed the victim was shot."

"Good idea," said Lew. "Thank you."

"And I will be happy to review these tapes with you again tomorrow morning before I leave," said Patience.

As she spoke there was a knock on the door and Officer Todd Martin poked his head in. "Chief, we've booked Wendy Stevenson. Searched her apartment but didn't find any of the missing articles—drugs, money, guns, jewelry—nothing. And she is not talking. You might have better luck with her than I had."

CHAPTER TWENTY

"I got the flu that's all," said the girl sitting across from Lew.

"Not sure the flu kills people within minutes," said Lew in a matter-of-fact tone. "You're lucky the EMTs had Narcan ready when they arrived or you and I wouldn't be sitting here." She gave the girl a long, hard look: "You know that."

The girl shrugged. The sullen expression hadn't left her face since Lew had begun the interrogation. "All I know is they didn't have my permission to use that crap on me and I'm going to sue the bejesus out of 'em."

Right then Lew knew she had an idiot on her hands. "Okay. Let's assume you had the flu, Wendy. Who gave it to you?"

Again the shrug and silence. Lew sat silent, too. Finally the girl shifted on her chair and said, "I told your people to call Pete Bertrand and he'll get me out of here."

Lew studied the document in front of her. "Yes, I see that Mr. Bertrand arranged for your bail the other day . . . "

"Told you." The tone was triumphant.

" . . . and you asked the hospital to call him this morning when you were admitted to the emergency room. But he hasn't returned their calls."

A flash of alarm crossed the girl's face before the sullenness set back in.

"So, I guess we wait for Mr. Bertrand. Is that what we do? Or . . . " Lew paused, "would you like to tell me why he's not calling to help you this time? Could it be he doesn't want to be associated with someone known to have abused a very dangerous and illegal drug?"

"He's busy is all," said the girl. "He'll call."

"Well, I'm glad you're so sure," said Lew, getting to her feet. "Until then you are under arrest for possession of controlled substances and theft. We'll talk more in the morning after your friend calls."

"Theft? What do you mean theft? You can't prove that."

Lew held up the container found in her purse. The girl averted her eyes.

"You mean I'm stuck here all night?" A string of expletives followed, which Lew ignored. She felt sorry for the kid. Wendy Stevenson wasn't the first girl they'd seen who'd been too gullible for too long. Lew hoped that she was right and her friend would call. The Loon Lake Police, the county sheriff, and the regional DEA office couldn't wait to get their hands on that guy.

———————

Resigned to spending another night alone, Osborne was busy stirring a pot of half-frozen pasta when Ray showed up at his back door, gave a quick knock, and charged into the kitchen. "Doc, I got the answer." He was holding something behind his back.

He spoke so fast and without the requisite torturous pauses that Osborne knew something big must be up.

"Glad someone does," said Osborne. "What? You've unlocked the secret to the universe? Or you know the exact moment walleyes will be spawning?"

"I know how to persuade Patience that I'm an okay guy even if I do fish—*and* she's coming to dinner at my place tonight. Fresh walleye caught, cleaned, and sautéed by these very fingers." Hands high, he wriggled his fingers.

"Isn't that living dangerously? Or has she changed her mind and decided fish *don't* have feelings?"

"Not . . . exactly. I . . . had the great good fortune . . . to stop by the Loon Lake Public Library to see if they have books on fish with feelings when . . . " he raised his right index finger, "the lovely librarian on duty . . . suggested I read a new book that just came in . . . on talking trees."

Osborne set down his wooden spoon and turned off the gas under the pasta. "Talking trees."

"Yep, talking trees." Ray beamed. "This guy in Germany has written a book about how . . . trees communicate."

"If you don't mind my asking," said Osborne, leaning back against the kitchen counter and crossing his arms while feeling like Scrooge about to tell a child there is no Santa Claus, "what do talking trees have to do with the feelings of fish?"

As he asked the question, Osborne wondered what it was in his life—his entire personal history as a health professional, a father, grandfather, and a widower known to enjoy fishing—that made it possible for him to ask such an absurd question?

"Here it is, Doc," said Ray, holding out the book he had been hiding. It was titled *The Hidden Life of Trees: What They Feel, How They Communicate.* "The end of the argument."

"I don't get it, Ray. I mean, what point can you make with trees that will change the woman's mind about eating fish?"

"Come on, Doc, think about it. If trees have feelings and we stop cutting them down, then we have no paper. No paper means no books and no books means no education. Right? You can make the same argument that a ban on eating fish has the potential for depriving millions of people . . . worldwide . . . of healthy . . . low-cholesterol . . . sustenance."

"Hmm, could work," said Osborne, suspecting "sustenance" may have been a word suggested by the librarian. But Ray's argument was not bad. He suspected, however, that Patience might have other reasons for not eating fish. Could be she simply doesn't like the taste of fish.

Ray was backing toward the door. "Ex-x-x-cellent argument, don't you think, Doc? Then . . . once she has a bite of my famous walleye . . . " The screen door closed behind him before Osborne could answer.

Turning back to the stove, he had to chuckle. Just wait until that young woman gets a look at Ray's bedroom with hundreds of fishing lures dangling overhead. That is assuming he is able to persuade her to enter a house trailer painted to resemble a predatory muskie: lurid green scales covering the outside of the little place and capped at one end with a row of gleaming razor-sharp teeth.

Osborne knew women often found his neighbor irresistible but would Patience Merrill? A woman skilled at looking beyond the obvious?

———•———

Realizing that spending the evening alone would give him a chance to complete his plan for Lew's workroom, Osborne reached for his most recent Orvis catalog. It was wedged between an old plat book and a plastic box of trout flies on the bookshelf behind his television. As he pulled it out, a framed photo, which had been shoved behind the stack, fell on the floor. Picking it up, he saw that it was one of Mary Lee's from years ago—a group photo of her bridge club. Seated at the table with his late wife was Harriet McClellan, a thirty years younger Harriet that is.

Her angular features and the haughty angle of her head brought back grim memories. While Harriet's stature may have shrunken with age, she still had that same mean look, a look in which all the lines in her face seemed to run downward. With a shiver, Osborne set the photo aside. He had the urge to toss it but knowing that his daughter, Mallory, was putting together an album of old family photos, he decided to show it to her first. She might want to include it if only as a record of her mother's love for the game of bridge.

Opening the catalog, he paged through until he reached the section on fly-tying supplies. While he knew that Lew had her own tools, he wanted to be sure to outfit the room so she wouldn't have to think twice before sitting down to work.

Ah hah, he thought, at the sight of a birch and cherry fly-tying desk—*that would be perfect.* He placed a check mark by the desk, then another check mark by a setup called a Regal Vise. He was getting excited at the prospect of surprising her with these. Another check by an item called the Ty Wheel, which would hold her tools in one place, and, finally, an epoxy dryer. Contemplating his choices, Osborne felt as pleased as he had when he'd caught a largemouth bass that May while fly-fishing with Lew up on a lake in Sylvania.

He circled the Orvis phone number on the back page and set the catalog aside. He would call in his order first thing in the morning.

CHAPTER TWENTY-ONE

Thursday morning was dark, wet, and gloomy. Pulling herself out of bed, Beth walked across the bedroom to look out the bedroom window. She was relieved to see wet pavement. Yippee—no tennis today. After three weeks of assisting the coach plus her early morning practices, she was ready for a break. She jumped back into her bed, pulled the light summer quilt up to her chin, and fell back to sleep.

She woke to music from her cell phone. "Beth?" It was Coach Moore. "Hey, kid, it's still overcast but I checked the courts and they're dry. Can you meet me here in half an hour? The boys' tennis team is coming to have their serve speeds checked with our radar guns."

"Sure," Beth managed, hoping she didn't sound too sleepy. "I'll hurry."

"Thanks, Beth."

There were six boys on the team and three radar guns on tripods. While the coach stood back watching the boys serve, Beth knelt at one side of the net to be sure the serves registered. Every few minutes she had to scoot in and adjust the guns.

When all the boys had been tested and it was nearly time for lunch, the coach apologized saying, "I'm sorry for the hassle, Beth. You're a good egg to help me out with this." He winced and said, "But I have one more favor to ask—" he checked his watch. "I'm supposed to meet my wife for lunch—it's her birthday. Do you mind putting the equipment away?"

"Of course not," said Beth. She grinned and said, "On the condition I get an extra half-hour lesson—just kidding."

"Kidding or not, it's a deal," said her coach as he jogged off to his car.

Humming happily, Beth gathered up the radar guns, slipped them into their cases, and headed for the storage shed at the far end of the tennis courts. She was on her tiptoes maneuvering the last of the boxes onto a top shelf when she heard what sounded like a squirrel skitter behind her.

She turned to scoot the darn animal out of the shed but the squirrel was six-feet tall, dressed in black jeans and a T-shirt that exposed ropes of tattoos running up both arms. That's all she saw before something hard landed on the side of her head.

———————

Beth had no idea how much time had passed before she became aware of lying on her side on the floor of a car that was bumping its way over rough road. With each bump she felt a stab of pain on the left side of her head. She tried to move off of whatever was hitting the side of her head but she was wedged in too tight. She opened her eyes but all she could see was the back of a car seat. A small wooden box was on the floor in front of her face and within reach of the driver. The fact she could see anything was hopeful: It had to be daylight still, though late in the day given the soft glow coming through the car windows. Maybe seven or eight o'clock?

Moving slowly in an effort to stretch out from the cramped position in which she lay, she realized that her wrists, ankles, and knees were taped together. Her mouth was taped but she could breathe through her nose. She stirred and found her feet could press against one side of the car. Only for an instant though as moving her head hurt so much she felt a wave of nausea. She fought it back, terrified of throwing up with the tape over her mouth. If that happened, she could die.

"I hear you back there, babe," said a male voice from the driver's seat. "Don't be a stupid girl 'cause we're gonna have some fun. Sorry to hit you so hard but it worked, didn't it?" He leaned his head to one side and gave a quick glance back toward her. "I didn't have time to talk things over with you. Got to make a delivery up north. I'll have big bucks after that. Spend a little on you if you behave."

The nausea swept up again. Beth held her breath, forcing herself to stay calm—if only she wouldn't vomit. At least she knew where she was: in the back of Pete Bertrand's Jeep Wrangler. He must have hit her with a flashlight or something to make her pass out long enough to get her into the car and tied up. Another bump and her head throbbed with sharp staccato bursts of pain—so painful she couldn't think straight. Not even to panic.

In a flash, she remembered a kitchen conversation between her parents, which she had overheard two years ago when her father was prosecuting a man who had kidnapped a ten-year-old girl. The girl had been able to outwit the kidnapper and escape unhurt.

The conversation popped into her head as vivid as if she had heard it moments ago: "That was one smart little kid," Beth could hear her father saying. "She played along with the creep no matter how weird he acted until he let down his guard and—bam—she was out of that van."

I will play along, thought Beth through the pain. *I will play along.* Closing her eyes, she felt hot tears pressing against her lids but she refused to let herself cry. *I will play along.* Steeling herself, she made a noise deep in her throat that she hoped sounded friendly. "Humm-humm?"

"Fun. Told you we're going north for fun." Pete twisted his head to stare down at her. "You feeling better?"

The nausea hit full force and Beth couldn't choke it back. Twisting and turning, she slammed her feet against the side of the car. Later she realized she must have looked like she was convulsing.

"Shit—" Braking hard, Bertrand jumped from the car, ran around to the side, opened the door, and yanked Beth out onto the grass. He ripped the tape off her face and hands and stepped back as she rolled onto her side and threw up.

"Are you all right? Are you all right?" he kept asking as she vomited again.

Beth lay back and took a deep breath. She reached up with one hand and felt the knot on her head. "No, I'm not all right," she said with short breaths. "Why did you hit me?"

"I had to—or you would have screamed." The bravado had disappeared from his voice.

Play along.

"I wouldn't have screamed," Beth whispered, afraid that speaking in her normal voice would make her head hurt worse. "I was going to call your friend, Wendy, and see if I could talk to you . . . "

"Oh yeah?" He seemed to think about what she had just said, then in a new voice, a voice with a more intimate tone, he said, "Y'know, girl. When you saw me yesterday and didn't squeal or run, I figured you might be up for something. Was I right? Huh?"

"Not sure now." Beth touched her head again. "I was going to see if you still wanted me to sell some weed for you but now I don't feel so good. Whoa, I'm going to be sick again." And she threw up. "Where's my purse? I need to wipe my face."

"Not here."

"My phone?"

"Nope." After helping her into the passenger seat, Bertrand handed her a clump of paper towels. "Here this'll help."

"What will really help is some ice," said Beth. "I had a concussion when I was a little kid. My toboggan hit a tree and ice really helped. Could we go somewhere and get some ice? Please?"

"Maybe. How about cold water? I'm on a logging road and we might go by a lake or a river . . . "

"Not the same." Beth thought she heard a hint of trust in his voice. The concern in his eyes when she was vomiting was real. Play along.

"How far north do we have to go before we find like a gas station?"

"I'm heading for Duluth to see someone," he said. "Once I'm north of Mercer, I'll get back on the highway." As he spoke he reached for both her hands and looped duct tape around her wrists.

"Not too tight in case I have to throw up again," she said.

"Yeah but I'm not taking chances."

Beth was quiet as he pulled the Jeep back onto the road. At least she was off the floor and her stomach seemed to be settling down. But her head was throbbing.

"Are we meeting Wendy?" she asked.

"Wendy's history."

"I like Wendy." Beth hoped this was the right thing to say. Make him feel good about his friend.

"She got old." He pulled the Jeep to a stop though he left it running and reached back into the wooden box she had seen on the floor. "Got some good stuff here," he said as he pulled out a small container, shook a powder into one hand, held it to his nose, and sniffed twice.

"Is that cocaine?" asked Beth.

"Nope. Oxy—crushed. Want some? Got plenty."

"I think I would throw up again. Maybe later?"

His eyes lightened as he gazed at her. "You might be okay," he said, sounding pleased.

Beth checked the digital clock on the dashboard. It was nearly nine o'clock. Her parents must know by now that something was wrong. Gingerly, she touched her head again. The lump felt like it had doubled in size.

CHAPTER TWENTY-TWO

At six o'clock that evening, as the family sat down to dinner at the kitchen table, Mark looked around and, spotting an empty place, asked, "What's Beth up to this evening? Still on the tennis court?"

"I have no idea," said Erin, "and I'm upset with her. She left the house around ten this morning in her tennis clothes and I haven't heard from her since. No note. No phone call."

"Are you serious?" asked Mark. "That isn't like her."

"Mark," said Erin, "she's fifteen. Who knows what a fifteen-year-old is thinking." She shook her head in irritation.

Midway through the meal, Erin set her fork down and jumped to her feet. "I'm calling Chrissie, see where those girls are. Beth knows she's grounded and not supposed to be out after seven. Kid is really pushing it."

After checking with Beth's best friend, Erin walked back into the kitchen. "Chrissie hasn't seen or heard from her. Said she texted her all afternoon and no response. Mark, this doesn't compute. I'm calling Coach Moore."

Another call and Erin returned to the kitchen, took off her apron, and said, "I'm driving up to the tennis courts. He thinks she may have decided to hit with some of the boys from the tennis team."

"*For six hours?*" Mark sounded incredulous. He looked at Mason and Cody, who had been eating quietly. "Guys, do you know where Beth might be?"

"She hates me. She doesn't tell me anything," said Mason, shoving another forkful of chicken and rice into her mouth.

"Me too. She told me I smell," said Cody. "Can I have some more milk please, Dad?"

"Brothers and sisters," said Erin with disgust as she walked toward the kitchen door. "Ain't life great. Mark, you coming?" Mark took one more bite of his dinner then wiped his face hurriedly with his napkin and nodded that he wanted to go along.

Pausing before getting into her SUV, Erin watched her husband open the door on the passenger side. "I'm worried, hon. Too many drugs in this town. I know she swore she wasn't one of the kids buying weed the other day but they are all too close to the action."

"And she's fifteen," said Mark with a grim look on his face.

"And she's fifteen," repeated Erin.

After parking near the tennis complex, Erin and Mark hurried along the walkway to the courts. Only two were busy, both occupied by adults playing doubles. They tried the door to the storage shed where they knew the tennis equipment was stored. The door was unlocked. Stepping inside, they saw a radar gun on the floor lying halfway out of its box.

"Over here in the corner, Mark. It's Beth's backpack, the blue and white one she uses for tennis."

"Are you sure?"

Erin reached into the bag and in a side pocket she found what she had hoped not to find: Beth's cell phone.

"I've got Chief Ferris's personal cell number in my phone," said Erin. "I'm calling unless you think maybe we're overreacting?"

"Maybe we are but what the hell," said Mark. "I don't like this. She's never without her phone. She sleeps with the goddamn thing for Christ's sake."

Lew and Osborne settled down for a late dinner on the picnic table outside her little red farmhouse. She lived on a lake too small for fishing boats, too boring for jet skiers, and so far from the lights of Loon Lake that Osborne had grown to treasure his two evenings a week at what he liked to call "Lew's Place": hours of peaceful silence, stars, and the warmth of her arms as he slipped off to sleep. Never in his life had he expected to be so lucky.

Both befuddled by yet another afternoon watching the Youth Fishing Tournament videos with nothing of note happening, they had left the police department early. Bruce was so frustrated he had decided that the spittle found in Chuck Pfeiffer's hair might be the key to who shot him even though Ray had protested yet again, "Bruce, have you ever noticed how many people spit when they talk without even trying to?" Bruce conceded that might be true but nevertheless he decided to run DNA tests on every single staffer who had worked in or *even been near* the Pfeiffer booth.

That made Lew happy as it kept him from bugging her. "I love the man," she had said, muttering, to Osborne. "I love that of all the Wausau boys I get to work with it's Bruce, but the guy's OCD habits can drive me over the edge. Let's hope it takes him the entire day to get samples from the Pfeiffer public relations staff and video crew."

Ray hadn't been a problem when they came up dry after running the videos the umpteenth time: He went fishing.

Lew sighed as she set a plate of spaghetti on the table and a bowl of salad on the table. "I have an early conference call with the governor's office in the morning. They want an update on the Pfeiffer investigation. On top of that, I continue to get nowhere with that Wendy Stevenson. She's refusing to answer any questions. I tried. Todd tried. She is one stubborn young woman."

"No luck reaching that guy she expects to post her bail?"

"Nope. He must be using a prepaid phone and I have no doubt he's determined to distance himself on this one."

She looked so forlorn Osborne decided to change the subject. "Love your spaghetti sauce, Lew," he said, scooping up a mouthful.

"Sauce is from last summer's tomatoes and the lettuce from this summer's garden. Pretty good if I say so myself." She smiled. They had a running joke that Lew never hesitated to compliment her own cooking.

"Did Ray ever convince Patience to eat fish?" she asked as she ate. "I forgot to ask him this afternoon but he seemed happy."

"Apparently she agreed to 'think about it' after his argument on talking trees. Also, she does eat shrimp but only because it's her mother's favorite dish and she doesn't want to hurt her feelings. But," Osborne raised his right index finger to mimic Ray, "she thoroughly enjoyed his wild blueberry pie with ice cream on the side. He told me he was smart enough not to mention that ice cream is made from milk, which comes from cows and cows have emotional issues, too."

He was still grinning when Lew's cell phone rang. "It's Erin," she said, looking at the screen. "Maybe she's looking for you for some reason?" Lew listened then said, "Don't take this the wrong way, Erin, but you may want to wait a few hours. This sounds too much like she may have run off. Trust me, she'll be back. I remember when my daughter—"

Lew listened again, her eyes darkening before locking on Osborne's, "I'll meet you and Mark at the station in fifteen minutes. Stay off your phones in case she tries to call."

Clicking off her phone and standing up from the table, Lew said in an even tone, "Doc, Beth is missing. She's been gone since this morning and they have found her phone and her backpack with all her things in it."

Osborne refused to hear what he heard. No. No. No. He sat stone still, fork poised. Beth? His beautiful Beth? The granddaughter whose face and eyes and cheekbones were identical to those of the mother he last saw at age six? How could he bear this?

"Help me carry the dishes inside," said Lew, watching him with worried eyes. "Just leave everything on the counter. We're meeting Erin and Mark at the station. I have to get out an APB as soon as possible."

CHAPTER TWENTY-THREE

Beth didn't know until her head bumped on the car door that she had dozed off. Waking, she became aware that the Jeep was parked somewhere with the motor running. Carefully she raised her throbbing head and tried to look around. Bertrand wasn't in the car but it was parked near a neon sign blazing The Wolf Den. She wondered how long they had been there. Glancing down at the clock on the dashboard she could see it was after midnight.

She twisted to get a better look past the steering wheel at the gas gauge. The gauge was so low they would have to stop for gas soon. Pulling and twisting her wrists, she felt the duct tape loosening. After a few more twists and tugs, the tape was loose enough for her to slip one hand out.

Peering through the darkness around the tavern and under the neon sign, she could see they were out in the country somewhere. Relieved that they were off the logging road and back on a highway, she wondered if this was the time to run. No, not good, she told herself. If the people inside the bar know Bertrand, they might help him, not her. Since she had no idea where she was, running through the woods in the dark might be dangerous. No, she needed a well-lit place with people, people who would hear her screams and help her. Knowing Bertrand was low on gas made her hopeful.

Beth slipped her hand back into the duct tape noose: She had a plan. Play along until . . .

The car door opened and Bertrand climbed in. He was carrying a small Ziploc baggie, which he tucked into the wooden box. "Hah," he said, "a buddy of mine just gave me some really good Oxy he got from Canada. *Really* good. He says anyway, but he was lookin' happy."

Putting the Jeep in reverse and backing out of the parking lot, he said, "Gotta get some gas down the road here. Get you some ice there, too. Soon as you feel better, we'll have fun. Promise." He winked.

"Thank you," whispered Beth. He patted her knee. She felt her insides curdle. She made up her mind to never ever let something like this happen to her again.

Half an hour later, he pulled the Jeep into the first convenience store with gas pumps that had lights on. Beth waited, watching as he walked in and appeared to prepay for the gas. She thought about making her move but the area around the gas pumps was so well lit that Bertrand would be sure to see her. Her indecision made her feel like crying.

Bertrand came out of the store with a paper sack and opened the passenger car door. "Here, babe," he said. He handed her a bag of ice. It felt like it weighed five pounds and was bulky and wet but she was happy to have it. She pressed it against the side of her head and watched while her jailer filled the car with gas.

Getting in, he set the paper sack behind his seat before reaching for the Ziploc he had stashed in the wooden box. Holding the Ziploc in his left hand, he drove the Jeep back onto the highway for a short distance until they reached a clearing along the road. Pulling over, he killed the engine, reached for a can of beer from the paper sack behind him, then slid his seat back and opened the Ziploc. He grinned over at Beth as he maneuvered a small funnel into the neck of a nasal-spray bottle and shook some of the powder into the funnel. After screwing the top back on to the bottle, he held it to his nose and snorted twice. Happy, he exhaled and relaxed back into the driver's seat.

He thrust the nasal-spray bottle toward her but she shook her head. "C'mon, babe," he said, "time for fun."

He grinned broadly and she was appalled to see two of his lower teeth were missing. Worse, the grin reminded her that all she was wearing were snug tennis shorts and a short-sleeved, tight-fitting athletic shirt. She knew her clothes were splattered with vomit but she doubted that would stop him. *Oh, God, what a creep,* she thought. But she knew as she shivered she would do anything to stay alive.

"Give me one more hour," she said, trying to sound encouraging. "This ice is working."

"Ah-h-h," he closed his eyes for a brief moment before sitting up so fast, Beth yelped in surprise. "Oh, sorry babe. Want to show you something . . . check this baby out."

He held out a small revolver. It had an ivory-colored grip that caught the soft light streaming in from the moon and stars. "Ain't she pretty?"

"Isn't that a ladies' purse gun?"

"Yep. Might be a ladies' gun but fits great in my pocket. Does what it needs to do, too." He turned the gun over in his hands and faked aiming it out the windshield.

"Nice. Where'd you get it?"

"Wendy. A parting gift you might say. I'll teach you how to shoot it."

"You don't have to. I know how. My grandpa taught me to shoot a twenty-two pistol. I'm good, too." Beth was determined to keep him talking about something other than her.

"You're okay, you know," he said looking at her, his eyes glassier than they had seemed in the daylight. Tipping his head back against the headrest, his arm went slack and he let the gun fall into his lap.

In the silence she heard him take a series of short, shallow breaths. His mouth fell open. She waited, expecting him to wake up with a start just as he had before. The minutes ticked by.

Cautiously she pulled one hand out from the duct tape. She felt for the door handle and clicked it down as she whispered, "Be right back. I have to see a man about a horse." No response.

She stepped out of the car and walked around to the driver's side where she opened the door to lean over him. The eyes were slightly open, no breathing. Her fear fell away.

Pete Bertrand was having fun somewhere far beyond the road to Duluth. Fun forever.

CHAPTER TWENTY-FOUR

Slumped in the armchairs surrounding the coffee table at one end of Lew's office were Osborne, Erin, and Mark. Arms crossed, Lew sat across from them. It was after midnight.

"I know my kids weren't getting along," said Erin, "but we're like any family that has a teenager, soon-to-be teenager, and a pesky little brother." She was repeating herself for the umpteenth time as she searched for a reason for Beth to run away. She *wanted* her daughter to have run away. That was so much better than . . .

Mark reached for her hand. "Honey, you've said that. And we know she hasn't been fighting with any of her girlfriends."

"What about that boy who was trying to buy the marijuana?" asked Osborne. "The one who got her in all the trouble."

"If you mean Kevin, Dad, forget it," said Erin in a voice verging on tears. "She got herself in that trouble. Don't blame her friends."

Lew walked over to her desk and picked up her phone to check with Dispatch. "No news, folks. Sorry."

Osborne did not like the sound of that: The APB had gone out before seven that night. Five hours ago. Problem was, he knew, they had no description of a car or a driver for whom to look. All that Lew had been able to offer law enforcement patrols across a three-state region was the fact that a tall, slim girl in her early teens wearing dark green tennis shorts and a white tennis T-shirt was missing. It was an impossible search.

Osborne got to his feet. "I'm driving out to the house to check on the dog. Call me if there's any change. I'll be back in forty-five minutes."

"Take your time, Dad," said Erin sounding despondent. "We'll be here."

"Doc," said Lew, stopping him in the doorway and resting one hand on his arm, "my gut feeling is things will work out all right. Beth is a smart girl."

"Lewellyn, I wish to hell I shared that feeling but—" Osborne couldn't finish his sentence. Feet filled with lead, he shuffled his way down the long hallway, out the entrance where Janine on Dispatch was sitting off to the right staring at her computer screen, and through the door to the parking lot. The fresh air helped a little.

———•———

Starting down the stone stairway to the lake, Osborne stopped halfway down to sit on the stone bench at the first landing. Ten years ago, when Beth was only five, the two of them would cuddle here on summer evenings and he would read to her from *The Wind in the Willows*. What would he give to have those moments back?

Moonlight glimmered on the gentle ripples flowing toward shore. Behind him was a muted chorus from oak and aspen, from maple and birch, as the trees rustled uneasily.

Resting his elbows on his knees, Osborne peered through the towering red pines guarding the shoreline like sentinels. His entire life those pines had confounded him: leaning *into* the wind, refusing to be beaten back, to be intimidated. If only he could harness their courage.

He must have sat there a good half-hour before getting into his car and returning to town. Back in Lew's office, he found his family tense and tired and refusing to leave even as dawn seemed inevitable and disappointing.

It was three thirty when the phone on Lew's desk rang and Janine on Dispatch demanded Lew put her on speakerphone: "She's safe," cried Janine. "I'm patching you through to a deputy sheriff up near Superior."

Everyone jumped to their feet and crowded around Lew's desk.

"We have a young person here who would like to speak with you," said the deputy on the line. He turned the phone over to a familiar voice. "Mom? Dad?"

"We're here, sweetheart. Are you okay?" asked Erin. Osborne held his breath.

"I am. I got a sore head and a big bump. I might have a concussion but that's all. I'm okay."

"Beth, what on earth happened?" asked her father.

Standing back from his daughter and her husband as they listened to their child, Osborne watched the color come back into their faces. He glanced at Lew and she gave him a slight smile. He knew he looked better, too.

Talking quickly Beth told them how she had been stalked by the boyfriend of the woman she had met when she was being held before being cited after the marijuana incident with her friends. She told how he had ambushed her in the storage shed at the courts and hit her in the head, knocking her out.

"His name is Pete Bertrand and, Dad, he OD'ed right beside me." That was as much as Beth could manage before sobbing.

The deputy came back on the line. "Mr. and Mrs. Amundson, Chief Ferris, we're going to take her over to the hospital and have her checked over but aside from a goose egg on the side of her head, she appears fine."

"We're on our way to pick her up right now," said Erin, talking over him.

"That's fine," said the deputy, "but we'll meet you halfway. That'll give us a chance to debrief her and there is no reason for you to drive all the way up here."

"I have a question," said Lew, "can you check the car that this Bertrand was driving? We had guns, jewelry, some cash, and drugs stolen from a nursing home here and the goods may be in that car."

"I did check it once," said the deputy. "Found one gun, fifteen thousand in cash, and a small amount of drugs. We think he was on his way to pay a supplier somewhere up near the Canadian border. We'll be testing the drugs because this guy OD'ed on something stronger than OxyContin—at least that's our theory right now."

"Please be sure I get a printout of the names on the drugs, please. I need to match them to the prescriptions stolen to be sure we don't have more floating around out there."

"Will do. We'll get you the girl, the guy's car, and its contents— and the drug info. What we need from you is more information on this deceased individual. He may be a drug addict but somewhere there is likely to be a mother who loved him."

"Or a girlfriend," said Lew. "Yes, you need next of kin and I think we have someone in custody who may be able to help us with that."

Later that morning, during the eight A.M. conference call with the governor's office, Lew and Bruce assured them that the investigation was moving forward. Off the phone line, they rolled their eyes at each other. "We *hope*," they said in unison.

Free of the conference call with the governor's staff, Lew and Osborne strolled two blocks to the Loon Lake Pub for a hearty breakfast after which she sent him off to get some sleep. It was nine o'clock when Lew walked into the cell where Wendy Stevenson was being held.

"Ms. Stevenson, we've located your friend, Pete Bertrand," said Lew to the young woman dressed in jail-orange and sprawled on the cell's cot with a pout on her face.

The pout vanished as the young woman scrambled to sit up straight. "Didn't I say he'd be in touch?"

"Umm, that's not quite how we reached him," said Lew. "He drove north with a friend of yours, Beth Amundson. Remember her? They were on their way to Duluth to meet someone. Did you know they were traveling together?"

"N-n-n-o-o." After a moment's thought, a classic "I knew it" look replaced the relief. She tightened her lips. Lew recognized the expression now crowding her features: revenge.

"Want to tell me where he lives? The more information you give me, the shorter your sentence. You'll be a cooperating witness."

"Sure." The word was spat out. "Out past the city cemetery and the old dump. You know where the Loon Lake Grocery has its bakery? Take that road a third of a mile to a house trailer. That's his grandmother's. He lives in the barn behind her place. You can't miss it."

"His grandmother lives there, too?" asked Lew. "Do you know her name?"

"Why? She didn't do anything. She doesn't know what he does either. Her name is Marge. That's all I know."

"We need to reach his next of kin."

Wendy's eyes widened. "Are you saying—"

"He's dead. Your friend OD'ed on his way to Duluth."

Stunned, the girl sank back against the pillow on the cot. "You should know, too, that Beth Amundson did not agree to go with him. He stalked her, hit her hard enough to knock her unconscious, tied her up, and abducted her. Do you have any idea why?"

The girl's face fell as Lew's news sunk in. She dropped her head in her hands before saying in a subdued tone, "Kind of . . . maybe . . . I told Pete I knew she was selling weed at the high school—so we thought she might be a good way in, y'know." Wendy raised her eyebrows as she said in a sad voice, "I knew he thought she was really pretty but I didn't think . . . " She didn't finish the sentence. Lew felt sorry for her. The tattoos alone would be a constant reminder of the man who deceived her.

Tired though she was, Lew made her way past the cemetery and the bakery to the small house trailer with the well-kept front yard. To the right of the dirt drive was an old barn with a well-trodden path between the trailer and the barn. The woman who answered the door was heavyset and mild-faced with wispy white hair, some of which was tucked into a knot on top of her head. Lew guessed her to be in her seventies.

"Mrs. Bertrand?" asked Lew. "I'm with the Loon Lake Police and we need to talk. May I come in?"

The woman stepped back with a nod but without saying anything. Lew walked into a small, tidy kitchen. Before she could say more, the woman said, "Bertrand was my daughter's name. She's dead. My name is Marge. Marge LeFevre. Is this about my grandson?"

"Yes, I'm sorry to have to tell you that he died sometime very early this morning of a drug overdose."

Marge closed her eyes and reached behind her for a chair. She sat down. "I knew this day was coming," she said, keeping her eyes closed and nodding up and down. It struck Lew she had had news like this before.

"I'm afraid I have to get some information from you."

"Of course. Please sit down."

Once Lew had the specifics, Marge said, "My daughter died of a heroin overdose years ago. I knew she was doing drugs but I couldn't stop her. Peter—I've always called him 'Peter'—was only three years old when his mom died. I thought Peter was with the man she'd been living with but turns out that guy went to jail and Peter ended up being moved in and out of foster homes. Some pretty bad. I didn't get him until he was fourteen. He was pretty messed up by then.

"He had his own reality is how I guess I would put it. Couldn't hold a job 'cause he would fight with whoever the boss might be. But lately he'd been doing okay. At least he stopped stealing money from me." She gave Lew a half smile. "You take a little kid who doesn't think he has a home and something has to happen. Problem was Peter had his way of doing things and once he set his mind to it—no changing.

"Funny thing though. He told me two days ago he had seen an angel." She nodded up and down. "Do you think he had a premonition?"

"Could be," said Lew, sympathizing but thinking of Beth. After explaining that there had been a burglary and she had a warrant to search where Marge's grandson had been living, Marge got to her feet. She reached for a cane beside the door and, walking slowly, led the way.

"I gave him the barn," she said. "He's been living there with that girl, Wendy. Now that girl—she's a strange one if you ask me. You met her?"

"She's in custody," said Lew. Again Marge nodded but said nothing.

Lew was relieved she didn't want to know more. Instead she motioned for Lew to follow her to the barn where she pushed open a door to one side of a barricaded entrance to the barn. "He got running water out here thanks to my late husband. He was my third," said Marge. "He's dead now but he put the plumbing in back when we thought we could turn this place into something.

"I've always thought it was a good thing he died before Peter got here. That would not have been good." Marge shook her head. "Ernie was a hard worker and he would not have put up with Peter."

Inside the barn, the living and eating areas were neater than Lew was expecting—as if a woman's hand had been at work. She suspected Wendy for all her goth décor was desperate for a husband and a home. She wouldn't be the first.

Behind the bedroom a door opened to the interior of the barn. Sunlight pouring through windows running along the walls made it easy to see Pete had been busy. One stall that had once held a cow was now the home of two flat-screen TVs, three laptop computers, a leaf blower, and two lawn mowers. Half a dozen expensive-looking bicycles, too.

In another stall and near a well-worn sofa was a cardboard box. Inside were fourteen handguns; a shopping bag filled with bracelets, necklaces, and earrings; and a large Ziploc containing vials of pills. Lew recognized names on two of the pill containers and realized the box contained the belongings of the residents of the Northern Lights Nursing Home.

Osborne woke from his nap, listened to Mike scratching at the back door to go out, and made a decision that brought a smile to his face. Before picking up his cell phone, he pulled out a credit card and the Orvis catalog with the list he had made two nights earlier.

Without flinching he agreed to overnight shipping. It meant he would have at least two days to assemble his purchases—just in time. Clicking off his phone he made yet another decision: He would host an early birthday dinner for the woman with whom he loved to watch sunsets. How could she turn down his offer after this surprise?

CHAPTER TWENTY-FIVE

Bruce Peters had promised to be back in Loon Lake early Monday after spending the weekend at home with his wife outside Wausau. When he hadn't called or shown up at her office by ten that morning, Lew reached him on his cell.

"Okay, Mr. Peters, are you holding out for another lesson in the trout stream?"

"Maybe," said the eager voice on the other end.

"I'm serious," said Lew, "if this is the only way I can speed up my access to lab results from you Wausau boys . . . "

"Not necessary," said Bruce, sounding chastened. "I'm running late like I always run late on Monday mornings. Sorry but I promise I'll be in your office in less than thirty minutes and I have interesting news."

"Good news? You've identified the shooter?"

"Umm, not that good but close. I'd tell you more but I think it'll be better if I can show you details on my laptop."

Lew clicked off and tried to focus on the paperwork in front of her. She was anxious to know if there had been any DNA match to the spittle found on Chuck Pfeiffer's head. Though multiple viewings of the video showed no sign of Rikki's motorcycle-riding ex, Jim Nickel, approaching the Pfeiffer booth, she kept hoping that a match to Nickel's DNA, which would be in the state's crime database since he had been in prison, might give them a "person of interest"—even if temporarily. Or enough to get the governor's office off her back. Some woman on his staff had bugged her twice over the weekend.

And while Patience Merrill kept underscoring her point that they could be overlooking something in the video of the crowd passing by Chuck, Lew could not imagine how that might be.

Off the phone, Lew called Osborne. She caught him in the midst of puzzling over the directions of how to set up the fly-tying desk, which UPS had dropped off early that morning. "Doc," she said, "looks like Bruce has an update for us—something to do with our Pfeiffer investigation. Wouldn't share it till he gets here but I'm thinking you might like to be in on this."

Osborne walked into Lew's office moments before Bruce arrived. He found Lew finishing up her phone conversation with the pathologist who had handled the autopsy on Pete Bertrand. Taking one of the chairs in front of her desk, he waited until she was off the phone to say, "Lewellyn, I still don't understand how my granddaughter ended up in that man's car. It doesn't make sense that he would just grab her off the tennis courts."

"I know," said Lew, studying the features of her dear friend as she debated how much to share of what she had learned from Beth. After encouraging the girl to get a good night's sleep after the long drive home with her parents, she had arranged for the two of them to meet in Lew's office late Saturday afternoon. No parents, no grandfather, just the two of them.

"Beth, I know there is more to the story," Lew had said without taking her eyes off the girl's face. "I don't know what it is but I want you to tell me. Even if it means incriminating a close friend, you have to tell me."

Without flinching, Beth sat straight, shoulders back, as she said, "No, Chief Ferris, no one else is responsible for what happened to me. Just . . . me."

"Okay . . . " Lew had waited, worried.

She liked the girl but she knew the hazards, especially the opportunity for bad judgment, of adolescence. Her own marriage at eighteen to a man who turned out to be alcoholic and abusive had been a disaster. Talk about bad choices. And she must have made serious parenting mistakes or why else would her teenage son have spiraled into the abuse of drugs and alcohol that led to his death in a bar fight at the age of seventeen.

She hoped her awareness of her own grievous errors in life made her a more compassionate law enforcement professional. Lew knew how easy it could be to do the wrong thing.

"Remember when I got picked up when my friend, Kevin, was buying that weed from the guy who met us behind the Loon Lake Market that day?"

"Yes."

"And I had to wait in a room with another person before I was cited and my parents were called?"

"Um-hum."

"There was a girl there, Wendy was her name. The way she was dressed, her hair and stuff—she was so *sick*." Seeing the confusion on Lew's face, Beth said, "I mean, she was what you and my folks would call 'cool.' Know what I mean? I feel stupid telling you this now but she made me feel like I was a nerd or something.

"And, um, when she told me she was in for something to do with drugs, she was so sick about it that . . . um . . . " Beth hesitated.

"I know what you mean," said Lew, "keep talking."

"I told a lie, Chief Ferris. I let her think that I had been caught selling marijuana so she wouldn't think I was a *total* nerd. That I was a stoner kinda like her even if I did play tennis." Beth gave a sheepish smile as if she knew how absurd it all sounded.

"Did she believe you?"

"Guess so because she and her boyfriend, Pete, drove by me the next morning when I was walking to the tennis courts and stopped to talk to me. They wanted to see if I would work for Pete at the high school—you know, sell weed. I said I wouldn't do that but he didn't believe me 'cause he came up to the courts again. Again I said no, absolutely not, but he wouldn't leave me alone. Made me sick to my stomach."

"So he knew where to find you."

"Yes, he stalked me for two more days. I could see him hanging out behind the courts."

"I wish you would have told someone."

Beth burst into tears. Lew handed her a box of Kleenex and when the sobbing had eased, Lew said, "I appreciate you telling me the truth, Beth. Now I understand how this happened." Lew leaned forward and patted her hand. "I wonder if you know how lucky you are. Something very bad could have happened . . . "

"I know. I know, I know." Shaking her head, Beth shut her eyes in an effort to squeeze back tears.

"Worse than what did happen. It isn't everyone who has to watch someone OD on drugs."

"I feel so bad," said the girl, wiping at her eyes. "What was I thinking? I'm happy to be a nerd, trust me." She gave a forlorn little chuckle. "Do you . . . am I going to be punished?"

"Listen, kid," said Lew with an understanding smile, "you've been through enough. This can stay between us. But I will need your help with one matter. The deputies up north will need you to testify that you witnessed Peter Bertrand entering The Wolf Den tavern without the Ziploc you've described and returning to the car with the Ziploc in hand—and that the powder that killed him came from that same Ziploc."

The relief on Beth's face was all the answer Lew needed.

———◆———

"Doc," said Lew, hoping she could give him an answer that would satisfy his confusion over why his granddaughter had ended up in Pete Bertrand's Jeep, "Beth and I had a talk Saturday afternoon. Turns out she met Pete Bertrand's girlfriend when she was here in the police station waiting to be cited after the attempted drug purchase behind the grocery store last week. The girlfriend misunderstood why Beth was being cited and she told Pete Bertrand that she thought Beth could be a conduit for selling drugs into the high school.

"Total fiction, of course, and when they approached her Beth let them know that was never going to happen. But Bertrand refused to take no for an answer. It's obvious he was quite attracted to her and started stalking her."

"Why didn't she tell someone?" asked Osborne, confused.

"I'm sure she thought she could handle it. That if she ignored those two, they would go away. There may have been some guilt in the back of her mind, too. Like if she hadn't been with her friend the day he was trying to buy marijuana that this would not be happening. Her mistake was thinking she was dealing with reasonable people who would take no for an answer."

"But he wasn't a reasonable person."

"Hardly. But Beth didn't know that. For a young guy—he was only twenty-one—he had a history of arrests for petty theft and domestic violence with former girlfriends. Some of his behavior I can understand after listening to his grandmother who tried to get him professional help. She shared with me that after the death of his mother, her daughter, the father had abandoned him when he was still a young child. He was shuffled through the foster home system until she learned what was going on and tried to rescue him. But the damage had been done."

"Poor woman. This had to be hard for her, too," said Osborne.

"Even though she's grieving, she has been very cooperative. Once Wendy Stevenson learned that Bertrand had planned to leave her and that he OD'ed, she's been helpful, too. Turns out she and Bertrand had been an effective little team burglarizing the homes of elderly people for whom she had worked as a CNA. I'm hoping Wendy takes the counseling she'll get while she's in prison seriously. Hate to have her die like her friend."

"What did Bertrand OD on anyway?" asked Osborne. "Heroin?"

"No," said Lew, "he inhaled a powdered OxyContin that had been mixed with fentanyl, which is ten thousand times as potent as morphine."

"Why on earth would you do that?"

"Doc, that guy had no idea the drug he bought was laced with death. He made the mistake of trusting his supplier. The DEA has said that even the suppliers don't know what's in the drugs they're pushing. It's a huge problem in this region.

"Enough of that," said Lew, her expression lightening as she slammed her hands onto her desk. "Enough about drugs and death. How 'bout a little good news for a change?"

"I'm ready for that and, Lew, thank you. You've helped me feel better about Beth."

"The good news," said Lew, "is that we've located pretty much everything stolen from the nursing home out at Pete Bertrand's grandmother's place. He was living in her barn and we found all the stolen property there—"

Before she could say more, the phone on Lew's desk rang. The receptionist at the front entrance let her know that Bruce Peters was heading her way.

"Chief—" One brief knock and Bruce walked through the doorway, his laptop tucked under one arm. "You will be so pleased."

"You got a DNA match to the spit on Pfeiffer's head—"

Bruce looked chagrined for an instant but he perked up. "No. But almost as good . . . " He opened the laptop and leaned over to set it on the desk and facing Lew. Walking around the desk to lean over her shoulder, Bruce said, "See this?" He pointed to the photo of a small handgun.

"I see that," said Lew. Osborne stood up and walked over to look, too.

"My good buddy in the ballistics lab got to work on the gun that was found in the car belonging to the dude who kidnapped Doc Osborne's granddaughter. You'll remember I asked the cops up north to courier that down ASAP? We wanted to see if it had been used in other drug thefts around the state. It arrived Saturday.

"Didn't turn up anything related to those burglaries," said Bruce. "But my buddy was sitting there with the bullet the pathologist had removed from Chuck Pfeiffer and on a whim he decided to check the ballistics on that sucker and . . . "

Osborne half expected Bruce's eyebrows to hit the ceiling he was so delighted. "Bulls-eye. You got your murder weapon."

"What? You're telling me this is the gun used to kill Chuck Pfeiffer."

"The very one. Ballistics testing showed a perfect match. All we have to do now is find the owner."

CHAPTER TWENTY-SIX

Elizabeth Herre was waiting for them in her office at the Northern Lights Nursing Home. She had the list of everything that had been stolen from the residents' rooms in front of her, including a description of the guns and their owners.

Before looking over the list, Lew said, "We have nearly completed documenting all the items, including the prescription drugs, which we hope to return to their owners in the next day or so. Right now we are particularly interested in the guns as one of them has been identified as the weapon used to kill Chuck Pfeiffer."

"You can't be serious," said Elizabeth.

"I am so serious that I've asked Officers Martin and Adamczyk to guard your front and back entrances in case the person of interest attempts to escape." After examining the descriptions of the stolen guns, Lew handed the list to Osborne. "Dr. Osborne, tell me if you recognize the gun and its owner . . . "

She waited while Osborne studied the list. The gun in question was an elegant Smith & Wesson Model 60 .357 Magnum firing .38 caliber bullets. Perfect for a woman's purse. The bullet that had lodged in Chuck Pfeiffer's skull was a .38 caliber. The owner of the gun was a former patient of his.

He looked up in disbelief: "Harriet McClellan?"

"Harriet McClellan?" echoed Bruce. "Did we see her in the video?"

"I don't remember seeing her," said Osborne, but even as he spoke the image of the small figure in black that had hurried over to greet Chuck came into focus in the back of his mind. "But we may have," he said. "We may have."

Elizabeth, who had been listening in stunned silence, said, "You don't have to worry about Harriet McClellan rushing out of the building. She isn't here. She has an appointment with her physician in Green Bay today. We have three residents who see specialists there so we arrange for a limousine—well, a nice bus really—to take them there and back. Because the appointments can run late we also arrange for them to spend the night at our sister facility over there. They are due back tomorrow morning. Around ten."

"Ten tomorrow? We will be here, too," said Lew. "In the meantime, Elizabeth, it is crucial that you keep our interest in Harriet McClellan and her gun confidential. Do not share what you have heard this morning with anyone on staff, a family member, *no one*. Have I made myself clear?"

"You have, Chief Ferris. Please, you can trust me to keep this confidential. If this news gets out, it'll be awful PR for my nursing home."

———◆———

As Bruce and Osborne climbed into Lew's cruiser to rush back to the police department, she hit the number for Dani on her cell phone. "Dani?" Lew asked. "We need to watch the video of the crowd going by the Pfeiffer booth again. We'll need to zoom in on certain images, too. Can you handle that? Or do we need to ask Mike, the videographer, to help us?"

"I can do it, Chief," said Dani. "Mike showed me how to work it and all the equipment is still set up. I'll have it ready for you."

"Great, we're on our way."

Lew, Osborne, and Bruce raced down the hallway to Dani's office. "Mike gave me the time stamp for the hour during which the shooting must have taken place. Is that what you need?" asked Dani.

"Yes," said Osborne, Lew, and Bruce simultaneously.

They sat in silence watching the crowd go by the Pfeiffer booth with some people greeting Chuck Pfeiffer with handshakes, others waving from a distance. Then the minutes—no more than two or three—when the figure in black wearing the wide-brimmed hat moved through the crowd toward Pfeiffer.

"Okay," said Bruce, "I see someone but I never see their face."

"I know. Whoever it is appears to be looking in the direction of Pfeiffer but that hat hides their face," said Lew. "I don't see a gun either, do you?"

"No, but arm movements . . . wait . . . *there* . . . " said Osborne. "See that glimpse of chin?"

"Yes. For a fraction of a second. What good does that do us?" asked Lew.

"That canvas bag or purse or whatever that is they're wearing could be holding a small handgun easily," said Bruce.

Half an hour later they gave up on the video. "Here's the situation," said Lew, crossing her arms and looking frustrated. "I do not have enough visual evidence from the crowd video to prove that Harriet McClellan murdered Chuck Pfeiffer."

Bruce and Osborne listened to her in silence. "It may be her gun that was used but if it was stolen once, it could be argued that it was stolen another time. Any fingerprints on the gun are likely to be those of Peter Bertrand and, maybe, Wendy Stevenson. It doesn't help that someone like Wendy and the rest of the nursing staff had such easy access to the resident rooms at Northern Lights.

"Add to that the fact that Peter Bertrand was dealing drugs. Chances are good he and Jim Nickel know some people in common given Nickel's time in prison and the halfway house where he had to come into contact with more than a few people connected to the drug trade. Who's to say he didn't hire someone to kill Chuck Pfeiffer using that gun."

"Could be he hired Pete Bertrand?" asked Osborne.

"I'll need to see a photo of this Pete Bertrand to see if he shows up in the video," said Bruce.

Lew sat thinking. "We just don't get a clear image of the individual approaching Pfeiffer. We can say it's her but we can't prove it."

"We have the shot of the chin," said Osborne. "I'm going to check my records for the work I did on Harriet years ago."

"And I'll get Bruce a photo of Bertrand," said Lew. "And we'll watch that damn video again." She sighed.

———

Once again Osborne was pleased that he had disobeyed Mary Lee when she insisted he destroy all his patient records. She had insisted that the two tall oak file cabinets, which held the dental histories of the patients he had seen over a thirty-year dental practice, were "worthless now and taking up space I need for storage in our garage. Paul, get rid of them."

He did—in a sense. One weekend when Mary Lee was on a shopping trip to Minneapolis with women friends, he and Ray had constructed a wall of sheetrock at the rear of the garage and behind the room where he cleaned fish, a room Mary Lee detested and never entered.

There he had installed the oak filing cabinets, their drawers packed with manila files: evidence of the career he had loved. Every once in a while, feeling nostalgic for those days, he would pull a file and see not just charts and clinical notes but a person, a human being whose face and voice he could recall in an instant.

He was confident that one of those oak cabinets held the file of a much younger Harriet McClellan. If he was lucky, the file might even have a photo showing her facial profile in a way that it might be matched to the image of the chin on the video screen.

———◆———

"Years ago I made a partial plate for Harriet," said Osborne, still thinking about the glimpse of chin on the figure in black. "Quite often I would take photos of the patient's jaw from several angles so I could be sure of the bite I needed to match."

"*You made Harriet McClellan a partial plate?*" asked Bruce, sounding as if that news was too good to be true.

"Yes. Why?"

"Jeez, Doc. If you could manage to check her partial plate while she is wearing it, we could get a sample of her saliva, which is an excellent source of DNA. Then we could check her DNA against the DNA in the spittle that was found in Pfeiffer's hair." Bruce turned to Lew, "Chief, we've assumed that the figure in black leaned over to cuff Pfeiffer on the head in a friendly way but maybe that's not what happened. Maybe it wasn't a 'good buddy' shove at all."

"Interesting. But that's assuming she still wears the same partial plate," said Lew. "Doc, how many years ago would you have made that for her?"

"Oh, it's been a while," said Osborne, struggling to come up with the year, "but up until I retired three years ago, I saw Harriet twice a year when she came for a cleaning and a checkup. She was wearing it the last time I saw her so I think it's safe to assume she still has it. Most of the dentures I've made for patients have held up well over the years."

"But, Bruce," said Osborne, "you're giving me an idea. Recently, there have been news stories regarding various medical devices that have not held up over time—"

"Yes!" Bruce's eyebrows jumped with excitement. "Might be time to see how that partial plate is holding up?"

"Yes indeed," said Osborne with a wide grin. The forensic tech's enthusiasm was infectious. "What if the plastic used in the partial plate is deteriorating?" asked Osborne. "Harriet needs to know that. I could arrange for her to get a new one from the young dentist who took over my practice."

"Okay," said Lew, "but how can we do this in such a way that Harriet doesn't suspect our interest in her?"

After pausing to think that over, Osborne said, "Assuming we don't want to alarm Harriet until we know if we have a DNA match, I suggest we arrange for me to visit Northern Lights to check the dentures that I've made for other former patients who may be residents at Northern Lights. I have recognized several former patients who are living there and this will be a volunteer effort on my part—"

"You got it, Doc," said Lew, interrupting. "I'm calling Elizabeth Herre this minute. I'll ask her to e-mail me a list of all the residents. I'll forward that to you and you can identify the people who have been your patients. We'll set up an informal session for you to stop by and check their dentures for wear. Tomorrow morning."

"At ten thirty," said Bruce, getting to his feet. "I'm calling my lab right now to let them know we'll be needing a rush on a DNA test."

Elizabeth Herre e-mailed over the list of Northern Lights residents and Osborne was pleased to see there were seven people on the list who had been patients of his. Four of them would be wearing dentures that he had made for them. On seeing that, Lew called Elizabeth again and explained their plan for Osborne to voluntarily assess the quality of the dentures he had made over the years.

"Would he mind checking other people who may not have been his patients?" Elizabeth had asked. "I know several who will be anxious to get his opinion."

"Whatever it takes," said Osborne. "I'm happy to help out." And he was for another reason. Lew might be the expert in the trout stream but he was tickled to be the expert in a field that could make her work as chief of the Loon Lake Police easier.

Before leaving Lew's office, Osborne asked, "Lewellyn, any chance we might spend tonight at my place?" Remembering the fly-tying table awaiting assembly, he half hoped she would say no.

"Oh, Doc, I would love to but my daughter and grandchildren are coming this weekend to celebrate my birthday and I really need to get my place ready. I've barely been home this last week. Can I take a rain check?"

"Your birthday!" said Osborne, hoping he sounded surprised. "I forgot all about that. Of course, I understand. Rain check accepted."

Rushing home, he fed the dog and hurried out to the garage and his dental files. Finding Harriet's, he went back into the house and tipped the contents onto the kitchen table. There were four photos but all were from angles that didn't show her chin as defined as the chin visible in the video. Certainly not good enough to be a match.

He had one other thought and walked into his living room where he had set the framed photo of Mary Lee's bridge foursome. Yes, there was Harriet with her haughty features sharper in those days. The woman's chin was thrust forward in what seemed to be a forced smile. Worth a try to match her chin with that of the figure in the video but it would be a long shot.

Disappointed, Osborne set to work assembling the fly-tying table and the rest of the equipment he had ordered. When he was finished, he stepped back, pleased. He went to bed happy that the room for Lew was looking quite good.

CHAPTER TWENTY-SEVEN

"Pay attention, everyone," said Elizabeth Herre, clapping her hands as she stood among the card players and television watchers crowding the Leisure Center of the Northern Lights Nursing Home.

"We have a treat for you today. Dr. Paul Osborne is here for one of our bimonthly sessions when local doctors and dentists volunteer to give us updates on recent advances in health care. Today, Dr. Osborne, who is retired from his dental practice, has made a surprise visit and he will be happy to give you advice on dental devices such as partials and bridges that you may have had for five years or longer.

"Specifically, he is interested in the plastics and other materials used in the devices as some have been known to deteriorate over time. Should your dental device need to be updated, he will provide a written recommendation for you to share with the dentist of your choice."

Osborne had set up a station for the exams in a meeting room nearby. Lew had stayed away, concerned that her presence might alert Harriet to their real reason for the session, but Bruce, wearing scrubs, stood by to assist Osborne.

So many of the residents were enthusiastic about the free check-ups that Osborne was taken aback. "I think I'll be here for at least two hours," he said in a low voice to Bruce as he watched people gather. The "limousine" from Green Bay had arrived shortly after ten but Osborne didn't see Harriet McClellan in the group gathering outside the meeting room.

He was about to ask Elizabeth Herre to check on the woman when Bruce jabbed him with an elbow. "She's here. Four more exams and we'll have her."

Osborne nodded then looked over the partial plate that he had just removed from one individual's mouth. "Looks fine. Not to worry," he said. He checked four more devices over the next fifteen minutes and then Harriet entered the room.

"Good morning, Paul," she said. "How nice of you to volunteer these exams. I'm sure my partial is just fine but never turn down a free checkup, right? Even if I won't be needing this much longer."

Osborne helped her into the armchair he was using for the exams. She was wearing a long-sleeved black linen jacket over a white blouse and dark slacks. The arm he grasped to help her into the chair was bone thin. "Harriet, I'm glad you made it back in time for this. I understand you were out of town."

While he was speaking she had opened her mouth and removed the partial plate. Osborne took it with one gloved hand and set it down on a tray where he and Bruce had set up the supplies that Bruce would need to protect the swabs once they held the saliva samples.

When Osborne had finished with Harriet's partial plate, he handed the tray to Bruce who left the room, anxious to complete the protocols that would ensure the swabs could not be compromised in any way before he could deliver them to the lab.

Jumping into his SUV, which he had parked at the rear entrance to the nursing home, Bruce was met by a Loon Lake Police squad car that followed him for six blocks before turning on its siren to escort him to the Rhinelander airport where the crime lab's helicopter was waiting.

For Lewellyn Ferris, each hour of the day seemed to stretch on forever. When Osborne offered to cook dinner, she accepted with relief. "Anything to make time pass faster, Doc. Oops, sorry, I didn't mean that the way it sounded."

"Not to worry, I feel the same way," he said, happy to share the lemon chicken and cheesy potatoes he had just slipped into the oven. Lew arrived at his place an hour later. Though he had closed the door to the room filled with her birthday surprise, she paced the house with so much nervous energy he found himself watching her as closely as he watched ground cover when hunting partridge. God forbid she open the wrong door and ruin his surprise.

———◆———

Late that evening Bruce called with the results from the crime lab. "Chief Ferris," he said, "thanks to a pushy phone call from the office of our concerned governor, the lab techs moved us to the front of the line. Once again it's helped that Chuck Pfeiffer was one of his biggest donors."

"Just the news, Bruce, just the news, *please*," said Lew.

"Oh, all right," said Bruce, pausing to relish the moment. "And . . . "

Lew listened. She exhaled. "Thank you, Bruce. And thank your lab team for rushing this through."

Turning onto her side to face the man in bed beside her, she said, "Set the clock for six, please. I need a warrant for the arrest of Harriet McClellan and I plan to be first in line to get that."

CHAPTER TWENTY-EIGHT

At nine thirty Wednesday morning, chief of police Lewellyn Ferris and Dr. Paul Osborne walked into the Northern Lights Nursing Home and asked to see Mrs. Harriet McClellan. The receptionist called the room number listed for Harriet, announced their arrival, and hung up. "She's expecting you. The hospice wing is down the hall and to your right."

"*The hospice wing?*" Osborne whispered to Lew as they walked down the hall.

"S-s-s-h, we're here."

Lew knocked and a reedy voice said, "Come in."

Harriet was alone in the sunny room. Resting against a bank of pillows, she was wearing a white nightgown with lace filigree surrounding the neckline. A tiny silver heart gleamed against the folds of pale skin around her neck. Her arms and hands lay still on top of folded bedclothes.

"Good morning," said Harriet with a welcoming smile. Osborne sensed a stillness about her that he had never seen before. Nor had he ever witnessed the genuine smile with which she greeted them. Smile aside, she was watchful, her eyes calculating as Lew approached the bed with the evidence case she was carrying.

Only when Lew opened the case did Harriet look down. "My gun. You found it." A bone-thin hand reached for the revolver. Lew didn't stop her. The old woman fondled the weapon. "This was a gift from my husband sixty years ago. He wanted me to have it for self-defense. That was never necessary. I got darned good with it, too, but all I ever used it for was to shoot gophers until . . . "

"Until you shot Chuck Pfeiffer." Lew's tone was even.

Harriet smiled again. "Yes, until I murdered the man who robbed me of all that was precious in my life." She couldn't have said, "I just won the lottery" and sounded happier.

The old woman's eyes met Osborne's. "You tell her, Paul. Chuck ruined Martin. Ruined him as a man, ruined his marriage and stole our business. He left my son crippled physically and emotionally. Martin was never the same after that . . . " Harriet's voice trailed off and she looked off as if the past were as vivid as the sunlight in the bedroom.

"Paul, help me sit up a little higher, will you please?"

Osborne plumped the pillows behind the bird-like shoulders and Harriet gave him a grateful smile.

Lew looked bewildered. What she had expected to be a tense confrontation had become a celebration. Harriet did not seem worried in the least by Lew's intent to arrest her for murder.

As if she could read Lew's mind, Harriet said, "You find this hard to believe? Don't.

"Years and years ago—I am eighty-seven, you know—I made up my mind that if I was ever diagnosed with a terminal illness that I would make it my mission to destroy Chuck Pfeiffer."

Again the smile of satisfaction, of genuine happiness. "And I have."

"I did not know you were ill," said Osborne.

"No one did. Not even the people here and I swore my doctor to secrecy. I was diagnosed with liver cancer five years ago but it went into remission until recently. Now, it's over. I've refused treatment and they give me three weeks at the most.

"But for those five years I watched and waited for my chance. When I saw that every year Chuck Pfeiffer attended that tournament and sat where he sat—every year the same spot. That's when I hoped I might have my chance. I never expected it to be so easy though."

"You were there in the Senior Center booth, right?" asked Osborne. "We've been watching a video Chuck's company was making and I thought I saw you there."

"Yes, I've gone with the group since the tournament started. Just watching and waiting. Two years ago I went over toward the Pfeiffer booth to see how close I could get. Chuck might have seen me but he didn't recognize me. I mean, it had been years since he saw me last. I've changed, you know. I am an old, old woman.

"Men like Chuck don't notice old ladies like me. This time when I snuck over to his booth, thinking I might have to fire from a few feet or so, all I had to do was reach over the railing and give him the old hug like I saw someone else do—and, what do you know? I was close enough to . . . "

Harriet held up her right hand and pointed her index finger—"Boom."

The room was quiet. Then Lew spoke: "Mrs. McClellan, you don't seem very ill."

"Good drugs," said Harriet, "but I'm failing. I can feel it."

"I'm sorry," said Lew, sounding uncertain as to what she should say.

"I'm not." It was the old Harriet: chin thrust forward, head high, eyes contemptuous.

"You spit on him," said Lew.

"I did. Waited years to spit in that man's face but I missed. Got the top of his head but so what." She gave a shrug of her emaciated shoulders. "What happens now, Chief Ferris? I have to go to jail, don't I? May I take this hospital bed? I promise not to be there long." Osborne swore he saw her wink.

Lew gave a slight smile. "We don't have a hospice wing. But I will have to arrange for a guard outside your door. A formality of the law."

"Ah, you think I might try to escape," Harriet chuckled. Osborne thought it might be the first time he had ever heard her laugh—a real laugh.

"Dear people," she said, "if I have learned anything in this long life of mine, it's this: You can't cheat death." Her eyes narrowed. "But you *can* settle accounts."

As they rose to leave the room, Osborne saw Harriet's eyes flicker and close. She was ready to sleep: exhausted but satisfied.

CHAPTER TWENTY-NINE

Dani looked up in surprise as Lew and Osborne rushed into her office. "Oh, thank goodness," said Lew on seeing the video monitor was still in place. "I was worried you might have taken the monitor down."

"No, I haven't," said Dani, "and I'm sorry. You told me yesterday that you might be finished with it but I've been trying to catch up with department records—"

"Not to worry, but can you help us with that third video again, please? Start with the time stamp we have for that period during which we were pretty sure that Chuck Pfeiffer had been shot."

"I know just where you mean," said Dani, speeding through the earlier scenes. She paused the video at the one forty-five mark then let it continue in real time. Lew and Osborne leaned forward in their chairs watching, waiting.

The figure in black appeared, entering from the far side and to the right of the busy walkway. "Yes! She *was* over in the Senior Center's booth," said Lew. "Doc, did you see her start to walk over?"

"S-s-s-h," said Osborne, "I'm concentrating." He watched as the figure moved in a diagonal line through the crowd and down toward the Pfeiffer booth. Her back was to the camera as she neared Chuck Pfeiffer, only the back of his head visible.

"I don't know if he even saw her coming," said Lew. "He didn't turn to look at her, did he?"

The figure they now recognized as Harriet McClellan turned slightly to her left as she neared Chuck Pfeiffer, her wide-brimmed hat obscuring her face from the video camera. For a second, Osborne caught sight of the canvas bag slung across her chest under a large black binocular case. Her right arm was not visible—she must have been holding it under the bag and out of sight of any one walking nearby.

Clad in a black sleeve, the left arm reached across Chuck's shoulders and the head under the hat leaned over as if to congratulate him on the success of the tournament. Chuck's head tipped back for a second in a move that appeared to be an acceptance of the accolade. Now the person in the hat faced him. To smile? Or to spit? Only the chin was visible as she gave his hair a friendly ruffle—an intimate gesture from an old friend—and moved on, disappearing into the horde heading for the dock to watch the awards ceremony.

"Doc, I'll bet you she was holding that revolver under her bag the entire time she walked toward Pfeiffer and no one even noticed."

"The binoculars are what caught my eye," said Osborne. "And the sound of the fireworks would have masked the gunshot."

"Patience was right," said Lew as she motioned for Dani to back up the video. "We see what we *want* to see. We walked in here this morning knowing what we *should* see—and now we do. Frustrating. No wonder they say the worst witness is an eyewitness."

"Ironic, isn't it?" said Osborne, relaxing against the back of his chair. "Chuck's people set out to make a flattering corporate history only to have it be a record of what can happen when you cheat the wrong person."

CHAPTER THIRTY

"Dad, wasn't it Henry James who said the two most beautiful words in the English language are 'summer afternoon'?" asked Erin as she helped Osborne finish mixing the potato salad for the picnic. Lew and her daughter's family would be arriving soon and he wanted everything ready beforehand.

"I think so," said Osborne, slipping the bowl his daughter had decorated with white and yellow slices of hard-boiled egg into the refrigerator. "Good, that's ready. Ray has promised to arrive early to sauté the walleyes he caught this morning and Lew insisted on baking her own three-layer chocolate cake even though it's her birthday. We're set."

Father and daughter walked down to the sandy shore by the dock where they had set up his picnic table. The blue and white checked tablecloth held paper plates, plastic cups, and napkins. The cooler with soft drinks and plenty of Lew's favorite Leinenkugel's Original beer was heaped with ice. In the center of the table was a wooden tray holding wedges of cheese surrounded with crackers.

"Looks perfect, Dad," said Erin. "Mark promised to be here by five with Cody and Mason."

Beth had come early with her mother and was back up at the house, sitting on the porch swing with a book. "She's been so quiet ever since we got her home. I'm worried," said Erin. "The whole experience had to be so frightening for her. The only benefit I see in all she had to go through is that she'll have a damn good story to write up for her college applications." Osborne gave his daughter a hug.

"Beth will survive," said Osborne. "She's got a good head on her shoulders. Like her mom. But that reminds me I want to have a chat with her before the others arrive." Osborne headed back up to the house, leaving Erin to shoo away a chipmunk with a taste for gourmet cheese and crackers.

With Beth beside him, they walked down the stone stairway to the bench on the landing where he had sat just days before, hoping and praying she would be found safe.

"Sit closer, young lady," said Osborne, pulling her into the crook of his arm just as he had when she was younger.

"Are you going to read to me, Gramps?" she asked with a grin. "Like you used to?"

"Not exactly." Osborne reached down for the gift he had wrapped and hidden under the bench that morning. "I have something for you." He handed her the package.

She unwrapped the book and held it in both hands. "Oh gosh, Gramps . . . *The Wind in the Willows*. My favorite."

"This is my copy," said Osborne, "the one my father said my mother got for me before she died. The same one I read to you. It's yours now."

She looked up at him. "But why—"

"Because. Just . . . because." Beth leaned her head against his shoulder. They sat quietly watching the lake. An eagle flew through the tops of the pines along the shore. In the distance a car door slammed.

◆

Ray strode into the kitchen and set a plastic bag of fish fillets in the kitchen sink. "Got a surprise for you, Doc," he said as Patience

Merrill came through the back door behind him. "Look who drove over from Neenah early this morning."

"Well," said Osborne, "looks like I better set an extra place at the table. That is if you are planning to eat with us?"

"I am," said Patience, helping Ray unpack his butter and flour and the paper bag holding the "secret ingredients" that he shared with no one and made his walleye fillets "more . . . special . . . than . . . the Good Lord's."

Osborne wasn't all that surprised to see her. Was there ever a woman his neighbor hadn't charmed? At least for a while.

"Doctor Osborne, I'm willing to give fish a chance," said Patience. "After what Ray told me about trees, I started thinking about the food I do eat—chicken, some beef, and pork."

"Cows have feelings, too," said Ray, rinsing his fillets under cold water. "And who knows how lettuce handles life." Patience gave him a dim eye, then laughed.

After Lew's chocolate cake and the French vanilla ice cream had been eaten, Ray asked Lew, "Chief, how did the Pfeiffer family take the news about Harriet?"

"Once Doc and I laid out the history between the McClellans and Chuck Pfeiffer, his family could understand Harriet's motivation but they continue to be surprised that she had the strength to carry it out."

"Hey, we all know the adrenaline rush that makes it possible for a mother to lift a car off her child who has been run over," said Erin. "On behalf of my family and our need to have a dad at the dinner table, I'm relieved that case is closed."

"Don't be too quick to close the books on the Pfeiffer clan," said Lew. "Watching and listening to Charlotte makes me wonder what's going to happen when that will is read. If Rikki Pfeiffer ends up with the controlling interest in the company and decides to move Jerry aside for her son, all hell could break loose."

"Oh, yeah," said Ray, "life in the Northwoods. Can I have another piece of cake, please?"

———————

Osborne walked Lew to her daughter Suzanne's SUV. He had already arranged for his birthday surprise to be delivered in privacy after all the family members had departed. "Date night tomorrow, right?" he asked.

"You're up to something, aren't you, Dr. Paul Osborne. Do I *have* to wait?"

"You sound like a little kid, Lewellyn. Yes, you have to wait." She gave a playful grimace.

Pleased with himself, Osborne returned to the kitchen to finish cleaning up.

CHAPTER THIRTY-ONE

Sunday lasted too long. Osborne had the new room ready by noon, leaving him with nothing to do but putter. First, he walked the dog up and down Loon Lake Road. Then he busied himself paying bills. Every half-hour he went downstairs just to be sure he hadn't forgotten anything but it all seemed just the way he wanted.

He had placed the fly-tying desk in front of the window overlooking the lake. A tall arborvitae shrub outside the house shaded the window from the sun, allowing dappled sunlight to stream in. On the desk was the Regal Vise, which had an imposing presence of its own. On a cabinet to one side of the desk he had set the Ty Wheel where Lew could arrange her tools alongside the epoxy dryer. The remaining shelves of the cabinet were empty— ready for fly-tying supplies.

The room felt open, spacious, welcoming. The fifth time he checked, he started to get nervous. What if he had been all wrong in thinking his idea would please her? What if she felt pressured instead?

He took the dog for another long walk.

Lew arrived shortly after six. "Since you insist on taking me out to dinner this evening, I brought dessert. Hope you don't mind leftovers," she said with a sheepish smile as she handed him a plate. "It's the last two pieces of my chocolate cake."

"There won't be any left over after tonight," said Osborne, taking the foil-covered plate from her. "Ready to go?"

"Really? Dinner already? I thought you were going to give me my present first." She sounded like a recalcitrant first grader.

"I guess we can do that," said Osborne. "But I forgot my wallet downstairs. Do you mind getting it for me while I call the dog in? Should be on the dresser in Erin's old room. I was making the bed up for Mason to use when she has a sleepover next week."

"Sure." He listened as Lew bounded down the stairs and walked to the room. He heard the door open. Silence.

"Doc. Come down here."

Hoping against hope, Osborne hurried down the stairs.

"Heck of a bed, you old man," she said, her eyes glistening with tears. "What are you thinking?" She walked into the room and ran her hand across the birch and cherry desk. "This is too much and too expensive," she said, touching the vise. Her eyes landed on the Ty Wheel and epoxy dryer. "Honest to Pete, *what are you thinking?*"

She stuck out her lower lip. "Please tell me you're not talking marriage again."

"No," said Osborne, "I know how you feel about that. What I am thinking is how 'bout this winter you spend four nights here instead of two. Won't this," he waved his arm around the room, "make it easy? Bring your own tools and supplies and work here?"

Lew thought hard, and while she did Osborne held his breath. "Okay, Doc. You are so thoughtful and I appreciate this. I really do but . . . "

His heart stood still.

" . . . how about a compromise? *Three* nights a week. Three nights a week I'm here, three nights you're at my place and one night a week we're each at home on our own."

"Sounds like a deal to me," said Osborne. She stepped into his arms.

That night, after sharing their favorite pizza at the Birchwood Bar outside Rhinelander, they walked down to his dock just as clouds impersonating flying saucers scudded overhead, backlit by moonlight. A light mist began to fall and they could hear a distant roll of thunder. By ten, as they were about to climb into bed, the rain was a steady drumming overhead. Lew paused to listen. "Doc, I love how we can hear the rain on your roof."

"Me, too," said Osborne. "Since I was a kid, I've loved the sound of rain."

He remembered how Mary Lee had complained, right after they had moved into the house: "Honestly, Paul, that builder did not insulate the roof very well. I can hear the rain. I insist you call him first thing in the morning."

"Certainly, dear," he had said and conveniently forgot to pester their builder.

The rain grew louder and as Lew folded herself around him he felt in the small of his back a shimmer of desire.

ACKNOWLEDGMENTS

Many people besides myself have worked to make this book possible: my editor, copyeditor, proofreader, page and jacket designers, publicist, sales reps, and booksellers—to name a few. But looking back over the history of publishing seventeen titles in my Loon Lake Mystery Series, I owe a special kind of gratitude to my publisher, Ben LeRoy, who has withstood the punishing realities of the book-publishing world today to keep Loon Lake on the bookshelf. Thank you, Ben.

Printed in the United States
by Baker & Taylor Publisher Services